THE LEAGUE OF 5;

OR,

THE LAST OF THE DALTONS.

LONDON:

17, GOUGH SQUARE, FLEET STREET.

THE LEAGUE OF 5;

OR,

THE LAST OF THE DALTONS.

———————

CHAPTER I.

ON THE MOOR—HARRY DALTON AND WILD DICK—THE COLUMN OF SMOKE.

THERE was sunshine on Rokely Moor and the warmth of late summer in the air as Harry Dalton, with his gun, wandered among the gorse, seeking, like the instinctive sportsman he was, for something to bring down with his unerring aim.

Harry was a few months on the right side of twenty, but in strength and manliness there were not many in that county of strong men—Cornwall—to compare with him. From his infancy the moor had been his home, and there he acquired a straight, stalwart form, abundant and unfailing health, and an eye that in clearness and power of vision was as that of the eagle.

He came of a race that had long dwelt on the moor. The Daltons of Rokely were an historical family, and the annals of the country contain many a story of their bravery on the battle-field. They left their mark upon the times of the struggle between Charles the First and the sturdy men under Cromwell, and later on through all our great wars.

Wherever the standard of our country was unfurled—in the Peninsula, at Waterloo, in the Crimea, or in India during the awful scenes of the mutiny there—a Dalton fought and bled and sometimes died.

Many a gap had been made in their numbers by the sword, or shot, or shell, until the time came when Stephen Dalton was left a widower with two sons, Harry and Cuthbert, one six years of age and the other a child of a few months.

Stephen Dalton lived practically a recluse at the Moated Grange, the old home of his race. There he reared his two boys, keeping them half hidden from the world.

He sought no society, encouraged no visitors, and kept few servants. Part of the Grange was kept closed, and into it neither of the boys had ever set foot.

Harry once asked his father for leave to enter it and see what it was like. He was answered only by a look, and that, in the case of Stephen Dalton, was sufficient.

The widely scattered inhabitants of the moor used to say that it were as well to stand in the line of a flash of lightning as to receive a glance of anger from the eyes of the owner of the Moated Grange.

Harry never referred to the closed portion of his home again in the presence of his father. On the moor he sought the recreation he needed.

Cuthbert, who was studiously inclined, spent most of his time reading at home. He was like the mother whom he had never known, and lacked the sturdiness of the Daltons.

The boy was not despised, but rather loved the more by Harry, for his delicacy. To the father, Cuthbert was the very apple of his eye.

In the early part of his life Stephen Dalton had been abroad, and from time to time indefinite legends of his doings there had been wafted across the moor. But they never reached the ears of his son, who, gun in hand, stepped onward through the gorse and bracken, joyous in the possession of youth and strength, thinking and fearing no evil.

Suddenly a dark object rose up in the hollow, and as quick as lightning the gun of Harry was at his shoulder, only to be dropped again with a light laugh.

It was the shock head of a ragged man that had risen, and next a wild face, tanned to the shade of an Arab of the desert, appeared in view.

"One of these days, Dick," said Harry, "you will have your head blown off."

"Aye, perhaps," was the reply, as the man rose to his feet, exhibiting a gaunt form of six feet three in height; "but it will be done by some whipper-snapper from the town, who fire first and think of what they are shooting at afterwards."

"A poor consolation that will be to you or any of us, Dick," said Harry Dalton. "Why do you lie close until a body is so near? With your ears you must know of one's presence long before he is within gunshot of you."

"I hear you—I see you when you are over there," returned Wild Dick, as he was called upon the moor, "but I am in no hurry. I have to watch and wait for their coming."

"For the coming of whom?"

As Harry put this question Wild Dick cast a sharp glance at his face and turned his head away.

"I watch for those who will one day come to the Grange," he said; "but the moor is wide, and I may not see them. If I am here, how can I mark them if they come from up the shingle side?"

"You are talking wild nonsense now, Dick," observed Harry, "but you are as sensible as any man in these parts."

"Master Harry," said Dick, "I know this. I remember some things, but not others. It was a knock of the head that scattered half my wits."

"Yes, Dick, I have heard so. You were abroad with my father at the time, but I never knew who did it."

"Who can tell you, Master Harry, when nobody knows?"

"But you know, Dick?"

A strange smile flitted across the face of the gaunt creature.

"Aye!" he said, "I know, but I will not say who scattered the wits of poor Dick. I live out here by myself, more wild beast than man, so that I may not be pestered by questions such as, 'Say now, Dick, who gave you that knock?' They worried me with it and drove me here. It was hard at first, but I have learnt to love the freedom of the moor."

"There is room enough for you at the Grange," replied Harry. "I have said so a hundred times. Why not come there? I'll see you are not pestered."

"I am coming back—*one day*," said Wild Dick, with a meaning smile, "and they will come too. I saw them last night as I lay sleeping in the spinney. They were on horseback—they were masked—and they had *done their work!*"

"I never heard him talk like this before," thought Harry, looking at the eyes of Dick, wild as those of a hunted wolf, roaming to and fro over the wild stretch of land.

Far away the Grange could just be seen, the outline of a toy upon the horizon, and here and there other lone buildings were dotted about—a wild, uncultivated scene, on which rested a sadness and the spirit of desolation, yet in its way picturesque and beautiful.

To Harry, who had seen little else of the world, it was always delightful. To him the moor was the fairest spot on earth. He had no longing to leave it, and would have spurned a suggestion that he should do so, and yet his days upon it were numbered.

The eyes of Wild Dick, after wandering here and there, settled upon the Grange.

It was, as we have said, but as a sketch of a toy—a little, insignificant break in the level of the horizon. Steadily the weird man gazed for a minute, or it might be more, and then, with a sudden scream of anger and terror, he leapt up in the air and darted off in the direction of the Grange.

The amazed Harry stared after him, wondering what it was that had led him to fly off in that startling way. In all his experiences of the eccentricities of Wild Dick—and they were many—he had never seen anything like this.

"Poor fellow!" he muttered; "he is getting worse and worse. I wish he could be taken care of. He used to travel with my father —confidential servant, I have heard—and yet he has never named him to me. I don't understand it. Perhaps Dick did something wrong, and— But I will not surmise; it doesn't help one anyway. Heigho! Meeting with him has put me a bit in the dumps. I'll have a smoke."

He threw himself down on the turf and brought out a pipe and pouch of tobacco. Having filled up, he lighted the narcotic weed and puffed away, trying to shake off an unwonted sense of coming evil that oppressed him.

But it could not be done.   The feeling was there and it lay upon him like lead.   The words of Dick, which on other occasions he passed lightly over, haunted him.

Was there anything in the wild expressions of the hapless man?

"It can't be," he murmured.   "Who in the wide world is there to come to harm us?   Or, if they did, are not the Daltons the people to give them a fitting reception?   It is nothing but raving on the part of the poor fellow."

Presently he knocked the ashes out of his pipe and turned his steps homeward.   He was going back earlier than he originally intended to do, yielding, in spite of himself, to the influence of a dim fear inspired by the language and manner of Wild Dick.

Grouse rose here and there, but he heeded them not.   Other objects for his gun crossed his path and were allowed to go scot free.   The heart of Harry was no longer in sport.   He was burning, without knowing why, to go back to the Grange.

Steadily striding on, he kept his eyes fixed upon the gables of his home, coming out clearer as he drew nearer.

"What is that?"

A thin column of dark vapour.

He stopped short and looked as it with keen eyes.

No ordinary smoke was this.   It did not come from the quaint old chimneys, for they burnt wood in the house, and smoke so black as this was never seen there.

Darker and thicker grew the column.   Harry's eyes widened, his nostrils dilated, and a feeling of terror, quite foreign to his nature, came over him.   A loud, hoarse cry burst from his lips.

"The Grange—*on fire!*"

If there had been nothing to lend significance to the sight it would have been sufficiently terrible, but with the weird warning from Wild Dick it opened up all sorts of alarming probabilities.

He broke into a run, and as, with fleet footsteps, he coursed along the moor, there cropped up in his mind many strange things he had noted and yet thought little of in connection with his father.

He, in particular, recalled one morning when a letter came with a foreign stamp and postmark, and the look upon the face of his father as he took it out of the bag.   Correspondence was very rare at the Grange, mainly consisting of communications from the agent or tenants of the estate.

Stephen Dalton did not read the letter in the presence of his son, but placed it in his pocket and left the room.

For days afterwards he had a troubled look, and Harry well remembered how he hovered round young Cuthbert, scarce leaving him for a moment, as if he had need of being closely protected.

At a run he hastened on, his gaze fixed upon the increasing volume of the fire.   No doubt now but what his old home was in the grasp of the destroying element.

And as he ran he saw two horsemen emerge from the drawbridge and ride towards him. Each had something strung across the front of his saddle, and their burdens were human forms.

It was evident that the men did not at first espy Harry Dalton, but presently, when there was about a quarter of a mile between them, they saw him and reined up.

A few words were exchanged, and then they put down their burdens and wheeled their horses round.

Harry, meanwhile, had been running with all the swiftness of a practised athlete, and was within range of the retreating horsemen. He now, for the first time, observed that they were masked.

On the impulse of the moment he yelled out for them to stop, and, dashing up to where the cast-off burdens lay, saw that they were the still forms of his brother and father.

The shock he felt was too great for him to experience its full force.

He was, in a measure, stunned, but the instinct to shoot remained.

Raising his gun, he took aim and fired, but, alas! it was with shot only the weapon was charged, and it scattered too much to do serious injury to the men.

One of them started in the saddle, but a shout of derision was the only response he received, and, breaking into a gallop, they rode away, leaving him with—the dead.

CHAPTER II.

CAN IT BE?—THE BURNING GRANGE—WILD DICK'S FRENZY.

ALONE with the dead !

Harry Dalton stood beside all that remained of the father and brother he loved—done to death, and that in the most cruel manner.

Around the neck of each was a cord, and the livid faces told the story of how they died.

Here the gallant father, who if stern was just—there the delicate brother, who had done no ill and thought none of living being. What was the meaning of this devilish work?

To Harry Dalton it was a puzzle that stunned him—a hideous dream. It did not seem possible that in a few hours a happy, peaceful life should be utterly wrecked.

He dropped his gun and knelt down beside the still forms. The manner of their death had made them hideous to the eye, and yet he saw it not. Here lay the father and son, who at early morn were alive, and now they were lifeless clay.

He laid a hand gently upon their foreheads, cold as ice. He spoke his brother's name, and the hapless boy did not stir.

He took out his knife, cut the cords about their necks, and endeavoured to restore them. But the light was out, and no mortal hand could bring it back again.

"Where was that Promethean fire
Which could the light restore?"

Not in the possession of man. The spark was out, and could not be rekindled again by living hand in this wide world.

He covered up the faces of the dead, raised his gun from the ground, and, with features as white and still as if cut from marble, set out for the Moated Grange.

As he approached the mansion he looked in vain for human being to hurry forth, or for further signs of friend or foe. It was not until he stood by the old drawbridge, used up to that day by the inmates of the Grange as a means of exit and entrance, ere there was a break in the terrible stillness and significance of the scene.

And then it was only Wild Dick who came bounding forth, tossing his arms, and crying—

"Too late! too late! To think that I should have watched all these years and miss them in the end. Oh! master, master, and you—young Cuthbert the peerless—where are you?"

Harry seized him by the ragged coat, and, at the peril of tearing it from his back, stopped him in his wild flight.

"Stand!" he cried, "and tell me the full measure of the iniquity that has been done."

"Master Harry!" screamed Dick, "is it you?"

"It is I," returned Harry, in a voice that sounded as if he were speaking afar off. "Collect yourself, Dick, and let me know the worst."

"In there," said Dick, with a wail, as he pointed to the thick of the flames, "all who served you are shut up, and roasting or being choked to death. Hear them—hearken to their screams rising above the roar of the fire!"

Fascinated, spell-bound by the further horror of the scene, Harry stood still, and above the crackling of the flames and the fall of burning timber he could hear the yells of imprisoned beings, doomed to die the most dreadful death.

There was no helping them, no appliances for putting out the fire. The moat was there, with water enough to swamp a dozen conflagrations, but not so much as a single bucket to put it to the needed use.

Harry sank down upon his knees and covered his face with his hands. Wild Dick capered about, uttering fierce cries, and that was an end of all they could do.

Higher rose the fire.

A gentle breeze drove it slowly on to the ancient woodwork of the rooms, where it caught hold like timber or matchwood.

Crash!

A portion of the roof was down, burying the habitable part of the Grange. And then there was a lull in the work of the fierce element. A million sparks danced up into the air, and the hot breath of the glowing mass warmed the cold cheeks of the kneeling youth, but there was no more flame.

"The foes of the house of Dalton prevail," yelled Dick, and, throwing his arms over his head, he again fled away.

Harry sprang to his feet and called after him—

"Come back and tell me the meaning of this."

"In the hour of vengeance," answered Wild Dick, stopping his headlong career, "I will return. Woe—woe to those who have shed blood to-day! Dark and deep the pit in which they shall fall and lie for ever."

Exhausted by his recent exertions, Harry could not have followed him even if he had desired to do so. Speedy as the hunted deer, Wild Dick resumed his flight across the moor, and his form faded away in the distance.

Afar off the fire had been seen, and the scattered yeomen of the locality, mounting their horses, soon came riding up, to find the last of the Daltons standing on the verge of the moat surveying the ruins, with a face that haunted them in their dreams for many a day.

They were a sturdy race of men, stout and strong, of simple habits, and all dumb at first with amazement. To them Harry turned, and his bloodless lips parting, he asked them if they could tell him who had done the cruel work of the day?

They had naught to tell him, but a white-haired yeoman coming to the front, said he had seen the masked strangers ride by, and they bawled out a message to the one remaining member of the house.

"Tell the proud young Harry that his hour, in turn, will come. It has been sworn that none of the accursed race shall remain."

"Why did you not stop them?" demanded Harry.

The old yeoman threw up his arms, an action expressive of his helpless state.

"I had only my riding-whip, and they were armed with pistols. What could I do?"

"Forgive me," replied Harry; "I did not think ere I put the question. You were powerless."

A score horsemen were there, and they sat in their saddles with the brows of angry men, who would have avenged the wrong done that day had they been able to do so. From one to the other Harry turned, his eyes ablaze with wrath.

"Friends and neighbours," he said, "in the past I saw little of you. It was the whim of my father to live alone, but now, in the hour of my extremity, you will help me to carry him away, so that he may not be left lying through the night upon the ground for the carrion crows to peck at. Come with me."

They turned their horses' heads, and followed him back to where the father and son lay still and horrible in death. And when they saw the cruel work that had been done each gave vent to his feelings according to his temperament.

Some wept, others brandished their hunting crops, and hoarse threats and oaths leapt from their throats. A few sat as men turned to ice, and made no sign.

"Who among you," asked Harry, "will bear them to the old church by the moor's edge?"

"Master Harry," said one, "they must be taken to the Pantin

Deer to await an inquest.   The law of the land stands good here as well as in more favoured places."

Two of their number dismounted, and each horse bore a corpse, which was laid reverently across the bow of the saddle.   The others fell in behind, and Harry, declining the offer of one of the other horses to ride, walked beside his dead brother, his right hand resting on the white palm of the poor boy.

And in this order they journeyed slowly across the moor, the yeomen exchanging whispers and Harry silent, but thinking.

In one hour all that he loved had been taken away from him. What had he now to live for?

Vengeance!

What had the past to do with the brother who had been done to death by a ruthless hand?   Whatever may have been the dark secret of his father's life, this delicate boy could have had no share in it.

"I live to find out the mystery of this wrong," Harry said, within his heart, "and whosoe'er may be responsible for what has been done to-day shall *perish!*"

———

CHAPTER III.

AT THE PANTING DEER—A QUEER LANDLORD—VOICES AT MIDNIGHT.

ON the verge of the moor, and standing at the side of the lone road, was an old inn, known as the Panting Deer.

Why an inn should have been built in such a place—where there were no houses within three miles of it, and not twenty homes in a radius of five times that distance—would offer a problem which the modern traveller would fail to solve.

To get at the cause of its erection we must go back to the days of smuggling, when such a place had its skulking frequenters lying in wait for the chance of "a run" from some lugger laden with excisable things.

At the time of our story it was kept by a man named Fang and his wife—a sullen, strange-looking couple, who existed no man around knew how.

They had been there for some years.

The inn was without an occupant for a long time when Stephen Dalton was abroad, but immediately after his return the Fangs took it, and there they had resided in practical seclusion ever since.

Whether their coming had anything to do with the Dalton family is a matter that will be solved by-and-bye.

On the day of the burning of the Grange and the murder of its inmates the inn was livelier than it had been for many a year, for it had five guests, two of whom were foreigners—one a Frenchman and the other a German.

The remaining three were Englishmen, whom we will introduce

to the reader as they sit in a room at the back of the inn drinking together.

Two of them were outwardly ruffians—one of gentle birth, the other a type of the country loafer, to whom poaching and thieving is a pastime.

The name of the former was Clewson and the latter Stork. In point of true ruffianism there was not much to choose between them, but for remorseless scoundrelism the born gentleman probably carried the palm.

The third man was of a different cast.

In his attire there was an apparent effort to look respectable. He wore black clothes, and his hair, also dark, was oiled and flattened to the sides of his head, after the style of men who desire to let the world see how good they are. So far his get-up was effective, but it was marred by a pair of villainous, sneaking eyes, and a nose that bore record to a long and steady devotion to the bottle.

There was no crime this man would not have perpetrated, but he was a cur at heart, and, unless it could be done with absolute safety, he preferred leaving it alone.

His two companions sat at the table with a swaggering air, but he had his legs tucked under his chair and his hands folded before him with all the meekness of a lamb.

Clewson and Stork drank freely when they raised the pewter pots to their lips, but he of the meek countenance took frequent sips, with the air of one who would rather not indulge, but, being in bibulous company, felt constrained to do as others did.

Clewson, after a long chat with Stork, turned his eyes upon the man in black, and gazed at him until the latter turned his head away with a smirk upon his lips.

"Swivels," said Clewson, sharply.

The man in black, thus addressed by name, started violently, and hurriedly exclaimed—

"Goodness! what is it now?"

"Goodness!" sneered Clewson. "What have you to do with that, you *worm*? I never look at you without feeling a strong yearning to wring your neck."

"Oh! don't," pleaded Swivels.

"Look at him," continued Clewson, "son of a church dignitary, a M.A. of Oxford, once private tutor to a nobleman, and now *dog* to a gang that have earned the gallows ten times over."

"He aint wuth looking at," growled Stork.

"Why do you always bully and worry me?" whined Swivels. "I don't want to keep with you. Can't you let me go?"

"No!" hissed Clewson, "for the first thing you would do would be to peach on the whole show. I am what I am," he added, as he fiercely smote the table with his fist, "but, by the light of the day, I owe it to you. Who fostered my vices as a youth for his own ends? *You*—you! Hang it! I think I *must* throttle you to-day."

"Mercy!" gasped Swivels, as Clewson rose to his feet with a savage air.

"Come, come," said Stork, pushing the other back into his seat, "there aint nuthin' in the wide world so idiotic as doing a bit of work without turning an honest penny by it. Sit down and let the stoat be."

"As he dragged me into the mire," continued Clewson, "so will I keep him there. Where I go there he shall follow. Every crime I have a hand in he shall share the danger of. If I hang, so shall he. If he wants to hang alone, let him say so ; it can easily be arranged for him. Say, you crimp, you viper, are you tired of your life ?"

The wretched Swivels dragged a soiled handkerchief out of his pocket and mopped his forehead, wet with the dew of fear. He opened his mouth and framed a further expostulation, but there was no sound from his lips.

"Go into the corner and sit there," said Clewson. "Keep as far out of sight as you can, for there is *red* in the air to-day, and I am dangerous."

Swivels got up, and, with shaky limbs, betook himself to a far corner of the room, where he sank into a chair and sat shivering, with his eyes fixed upon Clewson.

Stork said no more, and his companion, after muttering to himself awhile, became silent also.

The stillness became oppressive to Swivels, who, in the agony of fear that was upon him, felt that he must rise up and flee or scream for help.

At length there was a break in the silence.

Footsteps were heard outside in the passage, and the door being thrust open, two men entered the room.

One was a Frenchman, of square build, the other a German, of stout and heavy frame. Clewson and Stork sprang to their feet.

"How goes it ?" asked Clewson.

"It shall be done, and well done," replied the Frenchman.

"Vera weel done," grunted the German.

"Where are *they* ?" asked Clewson, with a strong emphasis on the latter word.

"Gone," answered the Frenchman ; "but it is, for all zat, *un fait accompli*, although we got them not."

"What do you mean, Rigault ?" asked Clewson.

"It vas said to us," replied Rigault, as he made himself a cigarette, "by you know who, 'Take dem avay—trow dem to de dogs and crows ; but on ze vay to do it—vat den ?"

"Ze cub vas on us," said the German.

"And so we drop dem," continued Rigault, "that vas vhy. Ask Hocknier vhy his heart went out."

"Dere vas two barrels," said Hocknier, sententiously, "to his little gun, and ve vas two—no more."

"*Pardieu !*" muttered Rigault.

"And, more," continued Hocknier ; "look at mine body, so big. He may not hit you, so thin as ze herring ; but for me—who shall miss ?"

Having put the matter thus, he drew out a big pipe from his pocket and proceeded to fill it.

"There is one thing about you, Hocknier," said Clewson, "which I never can understand. On horseback you do not look half your size."

"It is dis," replied Hocknier, calmly. "On my feet I am as brave as ze lion, but on ze back of ze horse I am not safe. It come to me zat I fear to fall off, and I *shrink*."

This candid admission raised a general laugh, and even the abject Swivels smiled. Hocknier lighted his pipe and smoked with the gravity of a judge who had just made some memorable remarks from the bench.

"All being done," said Clewson, "had we not better go?"

"At ze night, not before," returned Rigault. "Vould you ride into a prison in open daylight?"

"Suppose you have been tracked here?"

"Ve vas not followed."

"In that case the night will do," said Clewson; "but we must be on the sea early to-morrow, as there is sure to be a hue and cry. Did you ride straight to the inn?"

Rigault smiled.

"My friend," he said, "shall ze fox return straight to ze burrow? No, ve haf ridden wide. Ze horses are gone—zey haf ze stiff leg to-day."

The door now opened again and the landlord, a thick-set man with heavy features, appeared in the doorway.

"There are horsemen coming across the moor," he said.

Immediately all were on their feet, and looks of alarm were exchanged.

"Tracked!" ejaculated Clewson, between his teeth. "You have bungled it, after all."

"I svear ve vas not seen," returned Rigault.

"Only by one old man and ze little birds and flies," said Hocknier.

"But they are coming," urged Fang, "and you must prepare. No fighting. It can't be done. They are too many and too strong."

"We are all dead men!" groaned Swivels.

Clewson took up a pewter pot from the table and hurled it at his head. He ducked, and it flattened itself against the wall.

"So hot in ze temper," said Hocknier, serenely. "A volcano—a powder-magazeen! He is mad to have a red pokare so near him."

This was evidently an allusion to the nose of Swivels, which the owner of it resented with a malevolent glance. Fang, addressing Clewson, went on—

"You are too hasty. Lie close and quiet is the word. Here am I and my wife ready to swear that none of you have been out to-day. All you have to do is to sit still and know nothing."

"Goot," muttered Hocknier.

"A slow but sure friend," added Rigault.

Fang gave them another word of general caution and left the room, promising to return in a few minutes and report further.

As soon as he was gone Swivels was ordered out of his corner and placed between Stork and Rigault at the table.

"If he does anything to betray us," hissed Clewson, "*silence him!*"

They sat for a time exchanging a few words now and then in a low tone, all listening. After a short delay, but long to the expectant men, the landlord returned.

"In five minutes," he said, "they will be here. They walk their horses, for they bring the dead with them."

A savage exclamation sprang from the lips of Rigault.

"What said he of ze Grange?" he ejaculated. "'Go vhere you may, I vill haunt you.'"

"I can guess why they are coming here," said Fang; "it is for the inquest. You forget the customs of this country."

"Ah! so," observed Rigault, with a look of relief.

"But it must not be forgotten," continued Fang, "the whole country will be alive, and a crowd of the curious will be here until the verdict is given. You cannot leave until that is done. It would not be safe."

"Oh! Faderland," growled Hocknier, "it is not ze ting ve look for."

"Hark!" said Fang, "they are here. Listen! The hoofs of horses and the voices of men. Woe to you all if they suspect. There'll be no escape. They will make wisps of hay of you. But keep close and be dumb. That is your only chance."

He was gone again, and the five men sat listening for the entry of those who had brought the dead to the inn.

In a brief space of time the tread of heavy footsteps was heard and a murmuring of many voices. Deep-toned men were speaking, and the listeners, without the word of the landlord, would have known that it would go hard with them if the new-comers gained an inkling of their share in the dreadful work of the day.

"Keep close and be dumb," muttered Clewson. "Curse you! Swivels, get back some of your blood into your face. Must you *always* have your sins in capital letters written on it?"

But Swivels only groaned, and changed to a leaden hue about the region of his fiery nose. A ghastly, tell-tale companion was he for the evil-doers to have with them at such a portentous time.

———

CHAPTER IV.

HARRY AND HIS FOES—AN EXTINGUISHED LAMP.

IN the memory of man there had not been half so many people in the Panting Deer at one time as there were that day.

Ill news spreads fast, even in the most sparsely-inhabited districts.

The tidings of the fire at the Grange had gone abroad in the most marvellous manner, and the inhabitants of the country round were flocking in ere the dead had been at the inn an hour.

Harry Dalton took possession of a room on the first floor and shut himself in. There he remained alone with his grief until it was time to go to rest.

His bedroom was on the next floor, and it had the appearance of having been long without an occupant ; but thoughts of damp beds did not trouble Harry, and he undressed and got between the sheets. But he could not sleep.

The excitement of the day, the mystery surrounding the death of his father and brother, were all sufficient to keep slumber from his eyes. Half the night was gone when he sunk into unconsciousness, only to awake the next instant, as it seemed to him.

The room was quite dark, insomuch that he could not see a single object in it. He held up his hand, but it might as well have been lopped off for all he could see of it.

Hark ! What is that ?

Voices somewhere—not far away, and yet not in the room.

" Why not go to-night ?"

" Because it is not safe, I tell you. Wait until the inquest is over and the young lion has gone away."

Then there was a silence of some two minutes' duration, which was broken by a dry, sarcastic laugh.

" On my word," said a speaker, with the ring of education in his voice, " it seems to me that we are all children. Five afraid of one, and he a bit of a cub."

" Ah ! vell," replied a hoarse, guttural voice, " it is as vell to be afraid now as to-morrow. Ze coward heart live long. He who fight and run avay shall live to fight anoder day."

" Well, don't talk," said the refined speaker ; " there is no knowing who may overhear us."

An assenting grunt was given to this, and then silence set in again, and was no more broken.

Harry lay awake thinking over what he had heard, and the inevitable conclusion he came to was that the men who were responsible for his father's death were in the inn. It only remained for him to find out where, and then he could exercise what he considered to be his just right of vengeance.

And his was a vengeance that could not sleep.

Rising, he put on his clothes, and, with a revolver in his hand, stole softly out of the room. He had, of course, to grope his way to the door, and he found the passage, if possible, even darker than the chamber he had left.

He crept along until he was sure he was near the adjoining room, and then he stopped again. On a level with his eyes he saw the faintest possible pencil of light, which came through the finest of cracks in the panel of a door. Somebody, and probably the speakers he had heard, was there.

It seemed an age ere he heard a sound, but at length the stillness was broken by a muttered anathema from a man whom Harry had not previously heard. The tone of the man was that of a country ruffian.

"I can't stand it. Let us have a bit of a jaw. Who is there to overhear us?"

"If we knew we could silence him for good," was the reply of the more refined speaker. "Where did Fang say he put the young lion?"

"He won't say. In his opinion there has been quite enough bloodshed to-day."

"To the deuce with his opinion. I, for one, vote we look him up and complete the job we were sent to do."

"And have all the country raised, and not a ghost of a chance for us to get away. Bah! Clewson, I did not think you were such a fool."

The blood of young Harry ran fiercely through his veins.

Here were the men, without a doubt—now was the opportunity of avenging the bitter wrong of the day. It would have been a difficult task to get help, for all the inmates of the inn, saving these men, were most likely in bed, and the people who had been there earlier were gone home. Alone he must attack them.

Passing his hands softly over the panels, he traced out the outline of the door, and finally found the lock. A touch of the handle and he felt that the door was not fastened—with a rush, he was in the room.

"Stand!" he cried, levelling his weapon at the five startled men, whose identity the reader has, of course, recognised.

For a moment there was a silence, and then Swivels, with a howl, sprang to his feet and made for a cupboard behind him. At the same instant Clewson dashed over the lamp, and the room was immediately in darkness.

They were all on their feet, and Harry received a blow on the chest that sent him staggering against the wall. He fired two shots from the revolver, and by the instantaneous light saw four men making for the door. He sprang at them, but the door was locked and the key turned, making him a prisoner.

He threw himself against it, but it was one that had been made years ago to keep out excise officers if necessary, and it resisted his frantic efforts. He had soon to desist, and, feeling his way to a chair, he dropped into it with a groan.

"Foiled!" was all he could say.

Like all smokers, he had matches with him, and, striking one, he gazed around him in search of the lamp. It was lying broken upon the table, but he perceived there was a candle on the mantelpiece, and that he lighted.

Remembering the man he had seen rushing for the cupboard, he laid hold of the knob of the lock, and with a jerk pulled it open. Swivels was lying in a heap upon the bottom of it on a pile of odd lumber.

"Mercy !" he gasped ; "I have done nothing. I am only a poor, miserable worm."

"Get up !" said Harry, fiercely.

Swivels arose, and, groaning, held up his clasped hands.

"I have done nothing," he repeated ; "I don't even know who the men are. It was by a chance I was in their company."

"Who are you ?" demanded Harry.

"I am a tutor out of an engagement," answered Swivels, glancing covertly at the threatening face. "I came here to inquire if there was a family in the neighbourhood in want of an educated man who was willing to give his services cheap. Ask the landlord if it isn't so."

Harry looked at him steadily, and he was forced to admit that this was not the sort of man to commit such a daring crime as had been perpetrated that day.

"Why did you hide ?" he asked.

"You came in so suddenly that I was startled," was the answer. "I am a naturally nervous man."

"And you do not know anything of those men ?"

"Never set eyes on them until this afternoon. Ask the landlord if it isn't so."

Harry turned from him, and with the candle in his hand walked across the room to the door and closely examined it. The lock was inside, and with a suitable weapon could be broken.

There was a poker, one of the old heavy sort, in the fender, and he took it up with the intention of smashing the lock. Ere he could begin the scampering of horses' feet was heard outside, and with an angry exclamation he resumed his seat.

"They have escaped for a time," he muttered, "but the features of all are indelibly printed on my memory. It is only a question of time ere we meet again."

Turning to Swivels, he said—

"I shall leave you now, and I expect to find you here in the morning. If you evade me I shall know what to think, and the next time we meet beware of me."

He struck the lock with the poker, shattering it at a blow, and pulling open the door, returned to his room.

It was useless to think of pursuing the men who had fled, and undressing again, he lay down and fell asleep.

CHAPTER V.

AFTER THE INQUEST — WILD DICK APPEARS AGAIN — THE JOURNEY ACROSS THE CHANNEL—A DARING RESCUE.

ON the morrow the inquest was held upon the dead. Twelve good men and true were sworn in to give a verdict according to the evidence, but there was very little evidence on which to found it.

"Wilful murder against some person or persons unknown,"

That is the usual formula in these cases, and it was used on this occasion.

Then the court, held in the coffee-room, melted away, and Harry proceeded to make arrangements for the funeral.

The family had a vault in an old church lying across the moor about five miles away, and thither it was arranged the father and son should be borne on the following Thursday.

It was when all necessary things had been attended to that the mind of Harry reverted to Swivels, and he recalled the fact that he had not seen him during the day.

Swivels had fled, and Harry put him down as a minor actor in the tragedy.

Thenceforth it would be as well for Swivels to keep clear of the last of the Daltons.

Harry had several offers of friendly shelter from the yeomen around, but he declined them all. He preferred staying with the dead until they were consigned to the earth.

A dull day, threatening rain, was the one appointed for the funeral, and no sadder sight had been seen on the moor for many a day than the coffin borne along on the shoulders of sturdy yeomen, with its one mourner walking bareheaded behind it.

On reaching the grave another mourner was found in Wild Dick, who had cast aside his rags and procured from somewhere a suit of fustian, such as keepers wear.

It made a great change in his appearance, and but for the wild expression of his eyes he might have passed for a rational and rather good-looking man.

He stood bareheaded and still, and when the last sad office had been performed he alone remained with Harry by the side of the grave.

All those who had gathered there out of respec. for the dead or from curiosity went away.

" Master Harry," said Wild Dick, drawing up to his side and touching him on the arm.

Harry looked up, and at first failed to recognise him.

" Dick," he said, " what has made this change in you ?"

" I am going abroad with you," answered Dick.

" Abroad ! I have not said that I was intending to do so."

" But you *have* to go, Master Harry, for it is there we shall find them."

" Find who ?"

" *The men you want.*"

" I can't tell you the name of the place or where to find it," continued Wild Dick, passing a hand across his forehead, " but I shall know it when I see it."

" Ah ! my poor Dick," said Harry, " it is a wide world in which to seek a place you have forgotten, but you may come with me wherever I go."

They walked away together to the inn, where the obsequious Fang had prepared a dinner, of which Harry sparingly partook, and after him Wild Dick ate his fill.   Then master and man walked away across the moor to take a last look at the Moated Grange.

The fire had stopped at the first half of the building, which had been occupied.   The uninhabited portion had escaped.

Some of the inner doors were exposed, but they had all been securely boarded up with rough planking, and nailed so that it would require a strong man to break his way through.

"Who has done this?" asked Harry.

"It is my work," replied Wild Dick, proudly, "and it will hold good until we come again."

"Alas! Dick," responded Harry, "I shall never return."

"You will—you must!" said Wild Dick, with a flourish of his right arm, "for it is here that the end will come."

Harry only shook his head, and with a farewell glance at his ruined home, turned away.   They slept at the inn, and on the morrow early rode away on two hired horses, Harry exhibiting himself as a graceful horseman and Wild Dick sitting his steed like a centaur.

Their destination was London, to see the agent of the property the Daltons held in the metropolis.   Harry was going to draw a sum of money and make arrangements for further supplies when abroad.

He knew not where he was go'ng, but intended to wander here and there with Wild Dick, on the bare possibility of some discovery being made of the murderer's whereabouts.

A week was spent in making certain transfers of property and arranging for the carrying on of the agency, then master and man started for Dover and took the boat across the channel.

A strong breeze was blowing, and the sea was very rough.   Some of the greater sufferers from *mal de mer*, which is a stylish name for sea sickness, put off crossing for the day, but among the more daring was a tall, aristocratic-looking man, who spoke with a foreign accent, and his daughter—a charming girl of eighteen.

As Harry and his man went on board he saw the pair seated on the lee side of the funnel, the father smoking and his daughter engaged in some sort of needlework.

There was so much composure about the pair that they made a picture few would have passed without glancing at.

Harry was of the age when one of them at least would have some attraction for him.

He slackened his pace as he drew near them, and their eyes met.   A pleasing thrill was felt by both, but speaking was out of the question, the more so as the elderly father stared somewhat haughtily at Harry until he had passed on to the aft of the vessel.

It was the evening then, and night would soon be there.   All who were going being on board, the boat put out to sea.

It was when they got into the open that they felt the full force of the gale, and the steamer pitched and rolled in a fearful manner

All who had any tendency to illness vanished down below, and only Harry, his follower, and the two passengers by the funnel remained in the aft part of the vessel.

Two waves were now running mountains high—they never do, as a matter of fact, but they were of great altitude—and began to sweep over the fore part of the steamer, swamping the deck.

The spray soon drenched all who were there, but neither father nor daughter stirred. The one went on smoking and the other carefully executing her needlework.

But suddenly, without a moment's warning, there came a wave that in size completely dwarfed all that had preceded it.

It struck the Channel boat with a force that made it quiver from stem to stern, and, fairly flooding the deck, rushed aft.

It was all done in a moment, and Harry had no chance of giving a friendly hand. The water dashed upon the young girl, and, lifting her up, carried her over the side of the vessel.

A wild cry burst from her father's lips, but he could do nothing. Harry, on the other hand, no sooner saw the girl carried over the side than he plunged into the sea to the rescue.

There was just light enough for the captain on the bridge to see that two persons were overboard, and he immediately stopped the boat and reversed the engines.

Wild Dick, with frantic gestures, pointed out where Harry was swimming towards the girl, who was kept afloat by the aid of her dress, which was partly inflated with air.

With strong strokes he clove through the water, seized her round the waist, and turned.

Now came the task of final rescue.

A life-belt with a line attached was thrown overboard and carried out of his reach.

A second one was despatched with a better aim, and he grasped it.

In the roaring of the wind the voices were drowned, but that was no bar to the work in hand. It was not the first time those strong seamen had hauled in a half-drowned man or woman, and each knew how he could best help in the work.

Carefully Harry and the girl were drawn up to the vessel's side, and as they rose on the summit of a wave that broke against her they were hauled on board.

The father, with a glad cry, seized his daughter in his arms and carried her below. Harry was assisted to rise by Wild Dick.

He saw nothing more of the girl during the short passage across the Channel, but a card was sent to him on which was printed the words, "Prince Vaubertie," and beneath the name was added in pencil—"Accept a father's grateful thanks."

Harry thought it would have been more courteous if the prince had waited on him in person, but he was not so much concerned about that as he was about the girl.

He thought of her sweet face, and he longed to look upon it again.

Was that joy to be denied him ?

It seemed so, for the boat put into Calais Harbour, and the passengers, for the most part more or less in a state of collapse, went ashore.

Harry lingered on the quay with the hope of seeing the prince and his daughter, but they remained below.

He asked the captain if the girl were seriously ill, and received a reply that startled him.

" Not at all ; she seems quite well, and is talking with her father in the cabin."

What was the meaning of it ? Why should they linger there when all the others had gone ashore?

There was only one inference to be drawn, and that was they did not desire to hold any further communion with Harry Dalton.

" They are ingrate," he muttered, " and too proud and haughty to take the trouble to verbally thank me for risking my life."

Wild Dick, who had been standing by watching the movements of his master's face, revealed by the light of the flickering lamps, broke in upon his meditations.

" Come away, master," he said ; " there's nothing in her worth thinking of ; she is wicked—I know her well."

" I wish, Dick," responded Harry, as he turned impatiently aside and signalled to one of the many touts to pick up his trunk, " you would try and not talk nonsense. How should you know the lady ?"

" But I do," replied Wild Dick, earnestly. " It was ever so long ago when I saw her—years and years. It was at—" He paused, thought for a moment, and shook his head. " I can't remember when, but it was a long time back, and she has not changed a bit— not a bit."

Harry hurried on in the wake of the tout—a short, thick-set Frenchman, wearing a blue blouse and wooden shoes. It had not occurred to him to ask the man where he was going, but now he put the question.

" To the Café Corday, monsieur," was the answer.

It was, in reality, all one to Harry where he was taken, for he knew nothing whatever of Calais, but he was surprised to find how far the café was from the sea.

Through broad and narrow streets, up and down ill-lighted thoroughfares, now to the right, then to the left, and anon seemingly going back again, until at last the tout paused at the door of a house, above which a meagre lamp was burning, and said—

" Monsieur, we are there."

CHAPTER VI.

WITHIN THE CAFE.

IT was not the place Harry would have chosen for himself or what he expected to find. He stopped the man as he was about to enter with a touch of the hand.

"This is too poor a place," he said.   "I want a good hotel."

"Monsieur," said the man, "it is good inside.   Come and see. It is not here, by the wall, you wish to stay."

"Is there no other hotel near?"

"None, monsieur; and is not for my strength to carry the trunk back again."

"Go in," said Harry, impatiently.

The man pushed open the door and entered.   The two travellers followed, and found themselves in a handsome saloon, with velvet cushions around.

There were marble-topped tables, at which a dozen men, in pairs, were seated playing a game of dominoes.

Two or three glanced at Harry and his companion as they walked behind the tout across the saloon, but otherwise no notice was taken of them.

Passing through a swing door at the top end of the room, the tout ushered Harry down a passage and up a flight of stairs to a sitting-room above.

Like the saloon below, it was handsomely furnished.

"For monsieur," said the tout, "there is a bedroom adjoining; for his valet a chamber above. Say, then, is not the Cafe Corday good?"

"It will do," replied Harry, relieved to find himself in these agreeable quarters.   "Here is something for you, and be good enough to send the landlord to me."

It was a liberal gift Harry bestowed upon the man, and his eyes lighted up with pleasure.   As he paused at the door to make a final bow the expression of his face changed.   For a moment there was a look of pity upon it, and then he vanished.

"Well, Dick," said Harry, "what do you think of your quarters? Better than we expected, eh?"

But Wild Dick was apparently not satisfied.   He glanced round the room with the uneasy air of a dog who scents something suspicious, but is not able to define it.

"I do not like it," he said at last.   "Wood and velvet, master, are nothing; it is the flesh and blood that is good and bad."

"Well, go, Dick, and see what sort of place they will give you," said Harry.

Wild Dick went slowly and hesitatingly from the room, and shortly after, a tall man, neatly dressed in black, entered.   He had a long face, with dark, watchful eyes close set in his head, and when he spoke his voice was more like the croak of a raven than anything human.

"Monsieur, you wish to see me?"

"Yes, if you are the landlord."

"I have the honour to be in that position, and your most humble servant."

They were speaking in French, a language which Harry, without being a proficient, could speak fairly well.

He ordered dinner to be served as quickly as possible, and expressed a wish for Wild Dick to be well cared for.

"He is a little eccentric," he said, "but you will not heed that."

"Monsieur, it is not for me to heed his eccentricities," was the answer. "Permit me to show you your room for sleep."

He lighted two wax candles standing on the mantelpiece, and, having opened a second door in the room, took up one in each hand and led the way to an adjoining apartment.

"See, monsieur," he murmured, "all of the best. Yonder is the bath. Behold the window. If a fire, open it, and see the iron ladder fixed to the wall for escape. It is not far to go."

"The arrangements appear to be excellent," said Harry. "I am pleased. Let me have dinner as quickly as you can, and send up at once a pint of Chablis."

There was nothing in the place to which anyone could object, but Harry, on being left alone, was conscious of a chill feeling creeping over him.

There *was* something uncanny about the place.

As he sat drinking his wine he looked about him, and tried to find out what it was, but there was nothing which could give him a clue to the feeling upon him.

The furniture, the pictures, the decorations were all in good taste. Nothing—absolutely nothing—to which he could take exception.

He dined well, for the dinner was splendidly cooked. Wild Dick waited upon him, with a full knowledge of his duties, at which Harry marvelled, until he remembered that in years gone by his attendant had travelled with his father.

After the meal he dismissed him, and Wild Dick, as he left the room, paused at the door to say—

"Locks, bolts, and bars are good for sleeping men's safety. Master, look to the doors and windows."

The door closed, and Harry was left alone. He lighted a cigar, but after a few whiffs threw it into the grate.

"I am tired," he muttered; "that swim in the sea wearied me. I will go to bed."

He thought it rather childish to lock the door, but he did so, and then looked at the window which offered such a convenient way of escape in case of fire by the ladder outside.

He threw up the sash and looked out. Below was a small courtyard, completely hemmed in by houses, the windows of which were all dark.

A moon had arisen, and sent one ray of silvery light from behind two huge chimneys to the square below. All was silent and still.

"One night in this place will suffice," said Harry, as he closed the window. "I will go to-morrow."

He raised his hand to close the fastening of the window, and found it was gone.

It had been broken off, and with the assistance of a match he saw that it had been done long ago.

"Pshaw!" he said, "what a child I am getting. What is there to fear?"

He drew the curtains across the window, undressed, and got into bed.   He placed a candle and matches upon a chair close to the bedside, ready for immediate use if required.

Then he sought much needed sleep, but it would not come.

A feeling that it was almost impossible to close his eyes came over him.   More than once he discovered that he was staring hard at the blank darkness overhead.

So one, two, three hours passed, and he was still awake.

He judged it must be long past midnight, and the dreadful weariness of insomnia lay upon him like some huge weight.   There it remained, and no effort on his part would remove it.

" I'll have no more of it," he said, " but get up and dress."

He was half out of bed, and had not yet lighted the candle, when a slight scraping sound on the wall without fell upon his ears.

It puzzled him for a moment, and then it flashed upon him that somebody was cautiously coming up the ladder.

It offered a way of escape in case of fire, but it also was a convenience to those who wished to ascend to the room.

And then there was the broken fastening of the window.   Two and two make four, and there was a combination of things that pointed to evil.

" I have been lured into a house to be murdered," thought Harry.

He did not strike a light or make the least demonstration of alarm, but groped about for his lower garments and slipped them on.

Then he took out a revolver he had in his pocket, and was ready for action.

" I will not be murdered quietly," he said, between his set teeth.

The scraping sound grew nearer, until it was close under the window-sill, and then it stopped.   There was a long pause, and Harry, standing by the curtains, could hear the partly-suppressed breathing of the person outside.

At length the sash began to slowly rise with only the slightest sound, and when fully up stopped.

Another pause, and then the heavy curtains were parted, and a broad band of moonlight was let into the room.

Harry, standing within the shadow, saw the head and shoulders of a man silhouetted against the light behind him.   The features were just visible, and he recognised the tout who had brought him thither.

In a moment he had the man by the throat with a grip of iron, and pinned him down upon the window-sill.

The face of the wretch was turned upward, and the moonlight fell upon his staring eyes and quivering lips.   He could not appeal for mercy, as Harry held him in a grasp that choked him.

Harry had it in his mind to shoot him, but he would not fire upon a man so helpless, so he gave him a fierce shake and let him go.

Down he fell from the ladder, turning over once and striking the paving stones below with a terrible thud.

Harry, looking out, saw he had fallen at the feet of a man, who bent over him as if he could scarcely comprehend why he had fallen.

There was no anxiety expressed by this man—the air was that of cool curiosity, combined with heartless indifference.

Not satisfied with his first glance, he knelt down and examined the fallen man more closely.

" Dead !" Harry heard him mutter.

After the exclamation he looked up, and Harry, to his bewildering amazement, recognised the features of Prince Vaubertie.

CHAPTER VII.

CHASING A PRINCE—THE SHOT FROM THE HOUSETOP—HITTING THE WRONG MAN.

THERE is nothing more exasperating to us than to be treated with ingratitude by those on whom we have conferred favours. To Harry Dalton the conduct of the prince was inexplicable, unaccountable, and monstrous.

Did he not, at the risk of his life, rescue the daughter of this man from a watery grave ? And yet here he was, from some mysterious motive, conniving and assisting at an attempt to assassinate him.

The blood of Harry bubbled with anger as he thought of it, and, without pausing to consider the result of a meeting between them, he got out of the window and swiftly descended the iron ladder that was so good for those who had to escape from fire.

Prince Vaubertie did not wait to hear what Harry had to say to him. Without actually breaking into a run, he started off at so swift a pace that it required an active person to follow on his trail.

Harry went in hot pursuit, but the prince, instead of keeping in the more open thoroughfares, turned down a narrow, dark way, that seemed to be no more than a blind court.

Harry discovered that the passage led to a road on the other side of the houses. He saw nothing of the prince as he ran through the dimly-lighted narrow way, nor was he to be seen in the broader street beyond.

He had disappeared.

" Hang him !" muttered Harry. " It is just as well I did not lay a hand upon him. What a cowardly, ungrateful dog ! Can he be indeed the father of the beautiful girl I saved ?"

It was almost incredible, but it left no room for doubt in the matter. Harry had seen the face of the prince too plainly.

As he stood there hesitating he received another illustration of the perils by which, in the most mysterious manner, he was surrounded. From a housetop on the other side of the street a shot was fired, and the bullet, whistling by his head, struck the wall behind him with an ominous ping.

He backed into the shadow of the passage from which he had recently emerged, and feigned to hasten away by imitating the sound of retreating footsteps.

Then crouching close to the wall, he kept a sharp look-out upon the house from which the shot had been fired.

It was like the rest of the places around, shrouded in complete darkness. The front of the house was flat, and there were barren windows in it, which were like those of a deserted tenement.

There was not even so much as a blind to indicate that it was inhabited.

But the blood of Harry was up, and he kept his post for an hour without stirring ; then he saw the door open and a man emerge therefrom.

His form was wrapped in a long, thick cloak, but Harry had no doubt it was the prince, and he went in hot pursuit of him, with his revolver ready for action.

The street was long and comparatively straight, and the cloaked figure, walking at a brisk pace, seemed unconscious of the approach of Harry until his angry voice was heard.

"Turn, you coward and ingrate, and face me !"

The figure turned, and its right arm was raised. Harry, on the alert, had his weapon ready also. Simultaneously two weapons belched forth their flame, and the cloaked figure went down.

Harry had good reason to fear the coming of the gendarmes, attracted by the firing, and he stepped into a dark doorway to await the issue of the exchange of shots.

He was resolved, if necessary, to allow himself to be taken into custody and charged with the crime of shooting the man.

But no gendarme or any other person appeared on the scene.

There lay the still figure, and no creature came near. After a delay of a few minutes Harry emerged from his hiding-place and walked up to the fallen man.

He was lying on his face, and he had to turn him over to make sure it was the prince. He did it with some compunction, and started back with horror.

It was a stranger he had shot !

The man, although about the height, and bearing in figure a resemblance to the prince, was a much younger man.

"Merciful Heaven !" Harry exclaimed, "what have I done ?"

He had now to think of his own safety, for all explanation from him would hardly avail in such a case. How could he account for having shot a complete stranger !

The man was well dressed and he had the appearance of an aristocrat. His features were refined, and there was a military cut in the trimming of his moustache and hair. On one of the fingers of his left hand was a large diamond, glistening in a setting of gold.

"I must away out of this horrible place," Harry thought. "Would the morrow were come."

He retraced his steps with all speed, and on reaching the little courtyard beneath his window discovered that the body of the tout was no longer there.

Who had taken it away ?

That he was dead when Harry went in pursuit of the prince there was no doubt. The would-be assassin had pitched upon his head and broken his neck. Who, then, had removed the body?

"I am surrounded by mystery," thought Harry, as he climbed up the ladder.

He entered the room, closed the window, and sat down. It would be useless to think of any more sleep that night, and he resolved not to attempt it.

In the dark he passed the intervening hours, revolving all sorts of ideas in his mind without getting the least clue to the inscrutable mystery of the whole business. Not a sound broke the stillness until the dawn arrived.

Then people, probably menials, began to move about the house, and he heard the chattering of women's tongues and the banging of brushes and brooms about the corridor.

In due time he was aroused from his thoughts by a knocking at the door.

"Now for the development of trouble," he thought.

But it was only a garçon, who wished to know if monsieur desired any hot water and a servant to brush his clothes. Harry bade the man come into the room.

"Have you been long in service here?" he asked, as he closed the door.

"Monsieur," said the garçon, "it was given to me to come here but a few days ago. It was on Saturday last that I arrived."

Our hero removed his coat, and the man proceeded to brush it with the hand of an expert valet. He was a bright-faced, country-looking fellow, both cheerful and communicative.

"Is it for monsieur to stay here for long?" he asked.

"I am passing through Calais," replied Harry, carelessly, "and I do not intend to remain."

"Ah, monsieur, it is a pity, then. So good an hotel, so cheap, too, and so much good company at times. Why even to-night, behold, there is a concert and a dance. So many ladies who are beautiful—the daughters of the best people of the town. Why, it is for the maire to be there to-night."

"Indeed!"

"Yes, monsieur, and many of the richest merchants will honour the concert and ball with their presence. Monsieur would be doing himself a wrong if he did not stay."

"Well, I will see," said Harry, as lightly as he could. "May I ask you to see if my servant is stirring?"

The garçon would fly on wings to see, and he flitted from the room with swift, silent footsteps only to return speedily with the disquieting news that Wild Dick was not in his room, and had not slept in his bed.

"Monsieur must not be angry, for see, it is for the servant to be gay as well as the master at times. If he is a gambler he shall not lack a place in Calais where he might lose his money," said the garçon, smiling, with the most innocent of expressions on his face.

Harry knew not what to make of it. He was well aware that Wild Dick would not attempt to gamble. Possibly he may have simply been in a restless mood, and gone forth to wander in the moonlight.

He affected to treat his absence with indifference, and ordered an early breakfast in the saloon.

And not one word was said of the events of the night.

It was scarcely probable that the garçon had the least inkling of the tragedy which had been enacted.

Breakfast was served with an expedition that spoke well for the discipline of the café.

Harry was about to partake of it when Wild Dick appeared.

He wore the same apparel as on the previous night, and, judging by its condition, had not taken anything off.

His eyes were bloodshot and he walked unsteadily.

" Master," he said, " I have sought it everywhere, and have not found it."

" Found what ?" asked Harry.

" The house—*her* house, you know ; it was not so far from here."

" Dick," said Harry, " you speak in enigmas to me. I do not grasp your meaning. Collect yourself, and try to make things clearer."

" Master, it is here," said Wild Dick, touching his forehead, " and yet not here, for the mists— Be patient, and the time will came. I shall make it all out."

" Dick," said Harry, " go and rest awhile, and then we will begone. I have a special reason for not staying longer than I can help about here. There is something wrong with the people of this place."

" All wrong," whispered Dick—" not one but has the *mark* upon him. Master, we must away from here—far, far away."

Harry bade him sit down and eat, for once in a way, with him, as time pressed ; but Wild Dick would not. He wanted nothing, he said, only to get away.

His moods were so strange and variable that Harry would not press him further, and, feeling that he could not stay there any longer without running some indefinite risk, he rang the bell and asked for his bill.

It was promptly brought to him, and he paid it, with a liberal gift to the servant. Not a word as yet about the events of the night, and the landlord did not put in an appearance.

" Would monsieur like a carriage or a porter to carry his trunk to the station ?"

Thus inquired the bright-faced garçon, and it was the pleasure of monsieur to have a carriage.

After a short delay one arrived at the door, and Wild Dick took his seat upon the box with the driver. He was in feverish haste to get away, and his eyes wandered restlessly here and there ; but there did not seem any cause for fear.

The street looked better by day than it did by night, although it was none of the best.

A few men of the working classes were moving to and fro, and a solitary gendarme wandered up and down, dignified in his loneliness.

Harry as he reached the door, looked back into the hall a moment, and then he saw the landlord.

He had clearly taken the man by surprise, for he was regarding Harry with a look of hatred and malevolence that, for the moment, gave his face a demoniacal expression. But in an instant it had vanished.

"I trust monsieur has fared well," he said, bowing low.

"Better than I could have hoped for," replied Harry, with a dry smile ; "and your arrangements for escape in case of fire I especially commend. I have had a very pleasant time. Good day."

"I have the honour to take my leave of monsieur."

Then Harry stepped into the carriage and was driven away.

CHAPTER VIII.

ON THE SWISS MOUNTAINS—THE MAJOR AND THE MULE—
ARRIVAL AT THE CHALET—A MIXTURE OF GUESTS.

IT was two months later and the scene the valley of Zermatt, the hour noon, and a fierce sun sending its rays down upon a small party wending its way through a narrow pass, which for the time was like an oven.

The party was three in number, and each bestrode a mule, on which the heat of the day had acted as a developer of obstinacy, for neither adjuration or strong language, or the application of heavy sticks, would induce them to get out of a steady crawl.

The foremost rider was a short, military-looking man, with a fiery face and eyes that blazed with wrath as he alternately anathematised the animal he bestrode and hit it on various parts of the body with a malacca cane of extra stoutness.

The second rider was a handsome boy of about sixteen, who, while he spared not his mule, seemed to take things coolly. Indeed, there was at times in his eyes a gleam of enjoyment as he listened to the foremost rider and watched the energetic nature of his castigations.

The third rider was of altogether different mould. His face was pinched and swarthy, and he rode bareheaded. His attire was a single white, loose garment, that covered him from his head to his feet. Instead of shoes he wore sandals, which hung loosely to his feet, and gave him additional cause for watchful anxiety.

He was not anything near so violent in his treatment of his mule, but there was a quiet intensity in the way he used a thick stick about its head and body which showed that he was also irritated by its laggardness. About every hundred yards or so he had to get down to pick up one of his sandals and readjust it on his skinny foot.

"It is my opinion," said the foremost rider, "that these brutes have a deliberate idea of broiling us. Stir your bones, you—you—Get on !"

"It's no use, pater," said the youth. "You put yourself out for nothing. It's a waste of energy, and, besides, it's heating."

"But fancy Major Starbuck, of the 1st Rutlandshire, being defied by a mule."

"It *is* rough, I admit, pater. My heart quite bleeds for you."

"Tom, you are laughing at me."

"On my honour, no, pater."

"Then that thief Flowerpot is. Hi ! there, you scoundrel, what are you grinning at ?"

"No grinny me, sar," was the reply of the dark-skinned owner of the horticultural name.

"Let me catch you at it again !" growled the major, ignoring the denial. "Come up in front and make the running for my brute."

Flowerpot dismounted, and, laying hold of the reins, did his best to get on ahead ; but it was a long pull, if not a strong pull, ere he got into the van.

To the great satisfaction of the major, the foremost mule now put on a spurt, and the others followed his example. All went well, and then off came one of those unfortunate sandals.

"Me no helper dat, sar," said Flowerpot, as he nimbly dismounted. "Get him quicker, sar."

As he stooped to pick up the sandal, the major, whose mule had stopped dead, leant forward and gave his follower a most unmerciful cut with the Malacca cane. Notwithstanding the thinness of the garment worn by Flowerpot, the blow had no apparent effect upon him.

He calmly adjusted his sandal and remounted into the saddle.

"Wi ! wi ! Get 'long !" he cried, in a voice as shrill as that of a penny whistle. "You runny much, boy, and me give you good dinner."

Whether the mule understood the promise or was scared by the peculiarity of his voice is uncertain, but the beast certainly broke into a gallop, and its example was imitated by the other two.

Flowerpot curled his legs up, whipped off his sandals, and rode barefoot. The major tried to look dignified as he bumped up and down in the rough saddle with but moderate success, and young Tom, standing up in the stirrups jockey fashion, made the most of the spell of speed.

"Wi ! wi ! you sar—you mule. You go—me give you dinner !"

On, on they went, over the rough road of the valley, the mules putting in good work until the speed was more of a stampede than an ordinary gallop. Suddenly a sharp bend was reached, round which the mules, now on a level with each other, swung at a dangerous pace, and brought the party into view of an hotel, in front of which a number of visitors of both sexes were lounging.

Coming upon them as a complete surprise, the major's confusion was increased by the mule bestrode by Flowerpot cannoning against his, so that both were upset and their riders sent sprawling.

Tom Starbuck sprang off his mule as it was going at full speed and ran to the assistance of his father.

"Don't touch me," roared the major; "let me get hold of that thief Flowerpot. Give me an axe or something."

"Don't, dad," whispered Tom; "there are no end of people here."

Some had come up, and in a quiet, well-bred way asked the major if he were hurt. He recovered himself immediately, and became the gentleman again.

"It was my servant's fault," he said. "I rescued him from slavery in Abyssinia, gave him a comfortable home, and he repays me by wrecking my piece of mind. Where is he?"

Flowerpot was standing on one leg, adjusting a sandal, and the expression of his face would have melted a heart of stone. The major shook his fist at him and strolled into the inn.

As he walked up to the clerk's window to secure rooms and order something to eat he saw a young fellow with a handsome, thoughtful face selecting some cigars from a box. The major looked at him closely as again and again he inquired of the clerk the particulars of the apartments to be disposed of. Having finished that part of his business, he addressed the young stranger.

"May I ask if your name is Dalton?"

With a start the other wheeled half-round, so as to fully face him, and hesitated a moment ere he replied—

"You have my name correctly, but I do not remember having seen you before."

"Nor have I met you, that I know of," said the major; "but a brother officer of mine was a namesake of yours—Theodore Dalton."

"My uncle," observed Harry Dalton. "He was killed in the Indian Mutiny."

"I was by his side when he fell," said the major, with a troubled face. "He was a splendid fellow, and I owed him my life more than once. As a matter of fact, he lost his in endeavouring to save mine."

"I never heard of that."

"No, nor would you if he had lived. You Daltons are not fond of bragging, and there is something about you that is unmistakable. I recognised you as one of the family the moment I saw you."

They strolled down to the door together, where they met Tom just entering. He was introduced to Harry, who took to the boy instantly.

The major asked our hero what lucky chance had brought him at that time to Switzerland.

"I am here on a mission of vengeance," was the reply.

And then he told them of his father's and brother's death, and of his conviction that he himself was marked for assassination by some body of secret foes, who, save in the person of the five men he had seen at the Panting Deer, and the Prince Vaubertie, had not declared themselves.

Both listeners were absorbed in the narrative, which, as the major said, was more like a page out of an old-time romance than a bit of modern life.

"And you have seen nothing of your foes since you were at Calais ?" said the major.

"Nothing," answered Harry. "But I am conscious at intervals of being shadowed. I am at all times prepared for attack. In my breast here I carry twelve men's lives. I am now a sure shot with the revolver. Every day I practise quick firing at small objects, and I rarely miss anything I aim at by a hair's breadth. This is not boasting, but only part of my story."

"When are you going to practise again ?" asked Tom, eagerly.

"This afternoon," replied Harry. "My devoted follower, Dick, has gone to find out a quiet spot, where we can be alone. If you care to come I shall be glad of your company."

The major begged to be excused, owing to his morning ride having tired him, and his habit in the afternoon being, like that of Hamlet's father, to indulge in forty winks or more ; but Tom could do as he pleased.

Naturally Tom, who was a thorough boy, was very pleased to be a witness of any feat with firearms, and it was arranged that after luncheon they should adjourn to whatever place Wild Dick had chosen.

"You may wonder at my being so secret in the matter," said Harry to the major, "but the fact is, when in Berlin, my daily practice brought me the reputation of being a duellist, and that is a title I should not be proud of."

About three o'clock a party of four left the hotel. It consisted of our hero, Tom Starbuck, Wild Dick, and Flowerpot. The latter was sent with his young master by the major, to keep him from idling around and talking to the servants of the inn of matters that concerned others more than himself.

Flowerpot deferentially brought up the rear, shuffling softly over the ground, and eying Harry and his wild-eyed follower in a critical manner. He had a way of closing up his small eyes so that he bore the appearance of one who is endeavouring to bear pain without crying out, which he indulged in a score of times ere they reached their destination.

Wild Dick had chosen a rent in the mountain side, about a hundred feet deep. At the bottom of it was an abrupt turning, disclosing a further rift, which formed a perfect natural rifle gallery.

"Now you remain here," said Harry to Tom, indicating the entrance to the gorge. "You need not keep particularly still, but do not speak to me when I am firing."

He brought out a pair of revolvers and laid one of them upon the ground, and Wild Dick produced a handful of small pistol cartridges, which he laid on a slab of rock.

Then he walked up to the end of the gorge, and, picking up a stone, held it up between his finger and thumb.

Harry stood with his back to him until he spoke, and then, wheeling round, he, without a moment's hesitation, fired at the object. It was carried away from the thumb and finger of Wild Dick, who accepted the exhibition as a matter of course.

On Tom and the watchful Flowerpot the skill shown had a startling effect. Flowerpot's eyes bulged out of his head, and his mouth worked as that of a fish just landed from the water.

The next thing done was even more wonderful. Wild Dick held up a card about four inches square, standing fifteen paces away, while his master, in rapid succession, fired all the chambers of a revolver.

The first shot went clean through the centre of the card, but the others apparently did not touch it.

"It was good to hit it once," said Tom.

"I hit it every time," answered Harry. "Come and see."

Undeniable evidence of his having done so was given in the form of six flattened bullets which had in turn struck a rock behind in precisely the same spot. One after the other they had gone through the hole in the card without varying to a perceptible degree.

"It is the result of constant practice," said Harry, "and is to a certain extent mere trick shooting, but it will serve my purpose one day, perhaps."

"It is wonderful !" exclaimed Tom.

"To much goodee shootee," said Flowerpot to Wild Dick. "Me no say rude ting to him. No, Flowerpot not make him angry, like de major. *Him* not hit elephant."

An exclamation from Wild Dick caused Harry and Tom to wheel round from examining the rock where the bullets had struck. It was caused by the presence of a beautiful girl at the entrance to the gorge.

She was clad in the close-fitting skirt of a lady mountaineer, and carried an Alpine-stock in her hand.

The exclamation uttered by Wild Dick was followed by another from Harry.

The new-comer was Aurora Vaubertie !

CHAPTER IX.

TRUE OR FALSE?—HARRY BETWEEN TWO FIRES—AT EARLY DAWN.

"THIS is a strange meeting," Aurora said, as she advanced, holding out her hand. "When attracted by the firing I little thought I should find my gallant rescuer exercising his skill in such a remote spot."

Harry took the small hand extended to him and murmured a few words of greeting. He was too much taken aback to do more just then.

"You are surprised to see me," siad Aurora, "and I do not

marvel at that; but I knew you were at the inn yesterday when I arrived. I am travelling with a chaperon; my father is in Ceylon. He has some property there which requires his attention."

Harry, more than on the first occasion, felt the influence of this beautiful girl. The innocent expression of her face led him to fully believe that she had no share in the doings of her mysterious father.

She asked him to go on with his practising, but he said he must give it up for the day, and they walked back to the inn together.

Tom was quite forgotten, and he followed behind with Wild Dick and Flowerpot, voting in his heart all pretty girls a nuisance.

"Fancy giving up shooting for a doll!" he muttered. "Blessed if I can make some fellows out."

"What became of you when you landed at Calais?" asked Aurora, as they strolled along. "I was delayed in the cabin by feeling indisposed, but I hoped to have seen you and thanked you again."

"It was really nothing," said Harry. "I only stayed in Calais one night, and there I met with an extraordinary adventure."

"Indeed!" she said. "You must tell me what it was. It was amusing, I suppose?"

"She knows nothing," thought Harry, and then he told the story of that night, without making any reference to the prince, her father.

Aurora turned pale, and exhibited various phases of emotion as the narrative proceeded. Carried away by it apparently, she unconsciously clasped the arm of Harry and leant heavily upon him as they walked along.

It was not until they were in sight of the inn that she betrayed any knowledge of what she was doing. Detaching herself from him with a blush, she murmured that they would meet again at the dinner-table, and hastened on ahead.

As she entered the inn, passing out of his sight, her whole manner underwent a change. She became more of the woman, the innocent look disappeared, and a weary expression took its place.

Ascending the stairs, she went down a long corridor, and opened the door of a room at the far end.

It was a small private sitting-room, with one occupant— Hocknier, the German.

"Ach! mine leetle bird," he said, "and so you coom back. How is it?"

"I have seen him, and I have fooled him," she answered bitterly. "I have so far done my duty to my father and my race. What there is else to do must be done quickly."

"Too mooch haste the less speed," said Hocknier; "but it may be done soon. Vat you say to him is to lure him to a place you vill know of vhen Clewson comes. He vill be here to-morrow."

"Well, until to-morrow I will not think of it. What cruel fate it is to have to destroy one who gave me back my life when it was as good as lost!"

"Ah ! vell, mine child," said Hocknier, "it is not for ourself to choose. Duty—duty is ze vatchword."

Aurora turned away and walked quickly to the door.

"Until to-morrow I will see you no more," she said. "For yourself, I say, lie close, for if he sees you he will shoot you like a dog. I have seen such skill on his part to-day that I have only heard of before, and deemed it to be a fable."

She opened the door and went out, leaving Hocknier to his reflections.

"I shall not show mineself," he muttered, "but it is not goot to live so close in the room. I must haf mine pipe in ze open air in ze early morning."

It was a pleasant evening Harry spent at the hotel. The *table d'hote* was a gay assemblage of men and women, and he had a seat by Aurora's side. He saw nothing of the chaperon she had spoken of.

Later on they went out to look at the mountains by moonlight— a superb spectacle.

They were alone, and stood on the piazza looking towards the Matterhorn, on whose jagged heights the full light of the silvery queen was resting.

In silence they stood for awhile, and then his hand softly moved towards hers. As soon as she felt his touch she drew back.

"Not to-night," she said.

"Aurora, may I not tell you what is in my heart?"

"Not here," she said. "To-morrow, up there, if you will come with me."

She pointed towards the Matterhorn and vanished. The whole thing was a startling surprise to him, but a pleasant one withal. To-morrow she would hear his love story, and her desire for him to relate it among the splendours of the mountain was, of course, only the desire of a romantic girl.

Later on, when he was having a cigar with the major under the verandah, his mind was still dwelling upon her. After a long silence the major said—

"My young friend, will you take a bit of advice from an old campaigner?"

"I will listen to it with respect," replied Harry.

"You are in love," said the major. "Get out of it as soon as you can."

"I do not understand you, major."

"The girl or woman you have fixed your mind and heart on will lead you to perdition."

"Major, what do you know of her?"

"Nothing but what I have seen to-day."

"Then you will pardon me if I consider your advice somewhat hastily given."

"It is a matter of instinct," said the major, "but I am sure it is a correct one."

Harry rose up, and bowing somewhat stiffly, bade the major good night.

"The old fool, to interfere in what he knows nothing of !" he muttered.

Hot and angry and more disturbed than he cared to admit to himself, he retired to his room. Here he sat down by the window, and remained there thinking of Aurora until long after the hotel was at rest.

He had good cause to congratulate himself, as he thought on the love of Aurora, and yet he was sorely depressed.

There were shadows in the moonlight, and he fancied at times he saw forms moving to and fro. Suddenly one figure stood out boldly for a moment and then was gone.

It was the figure of his father.

Was it fancy only, or really a visitation of the dead?

Perturbed, he turned from the window, and, lying down in his clothes, he tried to sleep.

But he could not. The warning words of the major rang in his ears, and the form of his father, although unseen, seemed to be in the room.

Daylight came, and he arose. A walk in the cool of the morning would help to clear the cobwebs from his brain.

He opened the door to go out quietly, so as not to disturb any of the sleepers, and saw a man stealthily stealing down the corridor.

It was the form of the recreant Swivels !

Harry was in an excited frame of mind, and the meeting was unfortunate for Swivels. As soon as he saw Harry he uttered an exclamation of alarm, and ran towards a room further down the corridor.

Swivels dashed into it, and Harry followed. The window was open, and Swivels, with wild alarm, leaped through it as if he had been a harlequin.

Harry fired at him as he disappeared, but took no aim. It was done more to alarm than to kill the cowardly tutor.

There was a yell from below. Swivels had dropped upon Hocknier, having that pipe he had promised himself in the early morning.

CHAPTER X.

HOCKNIER'S FLIGHT—THE FIRST BLOW OF THE AVENGING HAND.

"You fool !" roared Hocknier, as Swivels leaped up again ; "vhat you make an acrobat of yourself for ?"

Swivels did not answer him, but bounded away, running with a swiftness not usually displayed by men of his years.

"Stop, ass !" cried Hocknier, as he arose and hastened after him —"stop and tell me vhat is ze mattare."

He did not look upward or he would have found the answer in the swift and quiet descent of Harry Dalton from the window. Intent only on checking the flight of his cowardly companion in crime, Hocknier waddled on until he was out of sight of the hotel.

Swivels had out-distanced him and vanished.

"Ach !" muttered Hocknier, as he paused and wiped his heated brow, "ze cur haf ze *deliberal tremen.* He haf drunk himself mad, and he vill talk of oder people's business in his dreams."

He stood looking ahead, with trouble on his face, until he felt a hand laid upon his shoulder. Wheeling round, he saw Harry Dalton and knew by the expression of his face that his time had come.

From red to white and to red again, the changes of his face showed the emotion he laboured under. Then, with an effort, he braced himself up and stood firm.

"So," said Harry, " I meet with one of you at last !"

" I know you not," replied Hocknier. " It is not for me to see you before."

" It is a pity that you should have a lie on your lips," returned Harry, "at such a time as this. Take your hand from your belt, or I will shoot you down. Even now I may give you one chance for your life."

Hocknier dropped the hand he was moving towards his belt, in which was a concealed revolver. Harry, who had his own ready for action, kept a close watch upon his movements.

" First of all," he said, "it is useless to conceal your identity. I know you. It was you and your companions who laid my home waste. Tell me why it was done."

" I haf noting to say," answered Hocknier.

" Who set you on ?" asked Harry, sternly. " Was it the Prince Vaubertie ?"

" I am not ze companion of princes," said Hocknier.

" And I say you lie."

" Ach ! so you say vhat you like—it is not for me to contradict."

" One last word," said Harry. " I have no desire to treat you as a principal if you will but tell me the truth."

" To tell the truth is not to save my life. Too surely shall it be zat I die. I die anyway, perhaps. I know noting, I say—noting."

" Then stand back," returned Harry. " When I give the word you are at liberty to use the weapon you have ready there. It is your life or mine !"

Hocknier stepped back slowly, his eyes on Harry and his hand ready to make use of the weapon he had in his belt.

He was horribly pale, but the man, villain though he was, did not exhibit fear.

" *Now !*" cried Harry, suddenly.

Quick as an expert shooting at sight, Hocknier whipped out his weapon and fired.

There was the scream of a bullet as it sped by Harry's head, but it had barely passed when another report was heard, and Hocknier fell heavily upon his face.

There was no exclamation, no startled movement of the body. He simply fell and lay there still.

Harry, himself terribly pale, walked up to the fallen man and turned him over.   His face was as calm as if he were asleep.

In the breast of his coat there was a small round hole, through which the bullet had gone straight to his heart.

As yet there was no stain to show that it had gone further.

" I would have spared him," muttered Harry, "but he had to die, because the band of villains is too strong."

He looked around him.   There was no living person in sight, and he walked back to the inn without meeting anyone by the way.

With the aid of a vine growing on the wall he climbed back to his room, shut the window, and lay down.   A feeling of utter weariness came over him, and he fell asleep.

From wild and troubled dreams he was aroused by voices and footsteps outside.   Rising, he went to the window, and saw four mountain guides—men who had been engaged to lead tourists up the mountains—with the body of Hocknier on a rude hurdle they had constructed of branches of pine trees.   Servants and visitors were pouring out of the inn, uttering cries of alarm and surprise.

Among them was Wild Dick, who walked over to the dead man and looked at his still face.   Then he glanced up at his master's window, and a faint smile passed over his countenance.

Of all there only one understood the mystery of that man's death.

They did not bring the body into the hotel, but carried it away to an adjoining shed.   The people returned, and the usual routine of the day was begun.

The bell was ringing for the breakfast of those who lived *table d'hôte* when the mayor of the district, in his robes of office, arrived. He was accompanied by several fierce-looking gendarmes, whose brains had for the most part run away into enormous moustaches. They all looked sagacious, but they knew nothing.

The first thing to be done was to see Aurora Vaubertie, in whose company the dead man had been on the previous day.

But, alas ! she had nothing to tell.   The unfortunate man was, so she said, no more than a messenger from her father, and she did not even have any knowledge of his name.

Then it was remembered by a garçon that Hocknier had been seen talking with an English monsieur, whose nose was of the reddest, and who had taken one of the cheapest rooms.

Then the monsieur was sought, and not found.   Hence it was clear to the mayor and the gendarmes that he was accountable for Hocknier's untimely death.

The two friends or acquaintances must have quarrelled—probably there was a lady in the case—and he of the reddest of noses must be found.

Until that was done who could go on with the investigation? Not the sagacious mayor, who was an Alpine stock maker by trade, and very busy just then ; therefore did he, by virtue of his authority, postpone the inquiry until the morrow.

The excitement soon abated at the hotel, and at breakfast very little was said concerning it. Hocknier was a foreigner, unknown to anyone there, and the death of a man abroad is not of much account to travellers.

Had it been an accident to a tourist while scaling one of the mountains there might have been more interest in it.

Aurora was at the table, where her beauty naturally attracted considerable attention.

Apart from that she was a vivacious talker, and at times rose to brilliancy in her repartee.

All the men admired her, all the women envied her, but she cared little for either. She was watching all the while for Harry Dalton, and he did not appear.

It was not until the morning meal was over that she came across him outside, dressed and ready for the expedition they had arranged.

He came forward and greeted her eagerly. She met him warmly. There was nothing in the bearing of either to show that one had slain a foe and the other knew that it had been done.

Wild Dick was not far off, but he held aloof from Aurora. She, however, observed him hovering around, and asked Harry who he was.

"My man—my faithful follower, henchman, or what you will," he answered.

"I do not like the look of him," Aurora said, after a pause. "He is not to be trusted."

"Ah! you do not know him," replied Harry, with a smile. "Poor Dick! He is a little wrong in the head, but he is right in the heart."

"You men have no insight into character," Aurora said, with a shrug.

The guides now began to put in appearance. A number of them had been engaged—some to take parties up the easier ways, and others to guide the more venturesome.

One young fellow was going to make an attempt to scale the Matterhorn, and he was the hero of the hour.

Well, Harry and Aurora were to ascend the Matterhorn too, but not to the summit, as that young aspirant hoped to do.

They were going up one of the lower spurs, a mountain in itself, and there he hoped to tell her a tale so often told by men to eager women's ears.

"We have no need of a guide," she said; "I have been there twice before, and know my way."

They stole away as they thought unobserved, but more than one pair of eyes were upon them.

Wild Dick marked his master's going and went after him, keeping at a distance. Major Starbuck saw him also depart, and muttered an anathema on Aurora.

"There is no good in the woman," he muttered. "She will lead him to perdition."

Tom and Flowerpot were together, watching the various parties getting ready for a start, and it was not until Harry and his companion were far away that the boy learnt he had gone.

"And with that dolly, too," he muttered. "Dad, what do you say to a bit of a climb this morning?"

"Not for me, my son," replied the major. "I shall sit here and have a cigar. If I want to see what is going on up the mountains I can take a peep through one of the telescopes."

"I must do something," mused Tom. "Here, Flowerpot, you come with me. We will do as much of the Matterhorn as we can together."

"Me no climb much, sar," said Flowerpot. "Me got no legs—only sticks. Me rader stop with major."

"Confound you!" roared the major. "I don't want you idling about here. Go with Mr. Tom, and mind you bring him back safe."

"All right, dad," said Tom; "I shall look after myself and Flowerpot too. Come along, will you?"

With a wriggle, a sigh, and a groan, Flowerpot followed his young master, who in his turn went on the track of Harry and Aurora.

"I feel vicious," muttered the boy. "It isn't the first time I've landed a chum and then had him taken away by some pink-faced girl. Hanged if I don't do my level best to spoil their fun."

And he *was* destined to spoil something, as we shall see anon.

CHAPTER XI.

ON THE SPUR OF THE MATTERHORN—NOW OR NEVER—TOM STARBUCK MAKES AN ENEMY.

HARRY sat on the top of a high rock, with a precipice that went sheer down a thousand feet within two yards of him.

A slip or a push would have sent him into a lonely and almost inaccessible gully, where he would have been smashed to pieces.

Behind him stood Aurora, with her troubled eyes fixed on the line of vast hills stretched out before her.

"So," he said, "you will not hear me, even now?"

"No," she answered; "it is better to be silent yet for a while. What do you know of me?"

"I only know that I love you."

"I ask you to consider what I *might* be. Think of the possibilities which your want of knowledge of me opens out. I may be your bitter enemy, for all you know."

He started and turned round, so that his eyes rested on hers, but the troubled look was gone instantly, and she was smiling.

If for a moment he suspected she had any share in the animosity of her father against him that smile dispelled the thought.

He looked away again, and there was a short silence. Aurora, with a noiseless step, drew nearer to him.

A fearful struggle was going on in her breast. She had what

she deemed a duty to perform, and the fact that it was a crime did not lessen the necessity for its being carried out ; but he had told her that he loved her. It was her nature to be all or nothing.

Nay, more, she knew that she was fast learning to love him in return, and by-and-bye she would be his slave.

"One touch," she murmured, "one thrust with these small hands of mine, and he is gone. Why not do it ?"

She was drawing still nearer to him, with a frozen look upon her face, when once more he turned towards her.

"Aurora," he said, "suppose we have an understanding. I will wait patiently for you if you do not tax me too severely. Indeed, dearest, I have a work to perform which must be done ere I can settle down—a work—"

He paused as the thought of her father, for the moment forgotten, rose up before him.

" If you ever learn to love me," he went on, hurriedly, "you must consent to give up all for me."

" It is not love in a woman," she answered, "if she does less."

"Home, father, friends must be abandoned."

" When I love you I will do all that you ask, but I do not love you yet."

Once more she was drawing towards him, and her white face was quivering with the emotions that racked her to the very depths of her soul.

She was very near to him now, and by stretching out her hand she could lay it on his shoulder.

After a moment's hesitation she put it forth and touched him.

"Harry," she said.

He heard her voice, so low and trembling, and it thrilled him. He thought it was affection that gave it the tone, so tremulous and husky. Little did he dream that she was bracing herself up to do a deed which could never be recalled.

With love in the heart of one and murder in the other, what a strange couple they were !

"Aurora, dearest," he said, as he clasped the small hand that rested upon him.

She felt that she must do the deed now or never. If once he embraced her she would yield, and in her case to yield was to love a little while and then find death.

For those with whom she was linked would never spare her. Not even the father, who was so proud of his beautiful daughter, would have mercy upon her.

No, the man she was learning to love must die, and the next moment Harry Dalton would have been rolling down to the valley of death below but for a most unexpected interruption.

"Hallo ! Mr. Dalton. So I have found you. What plaguey work it is climbing these hills."

It was Tom Starbuck, flushed with the haste he had made to reach the top of the spur, and fully bent on spoiling Harry's " fun " with that pink-faced girl.

His coming was an interruption unwelcome to both, and he was favoured with a cool reception from Harry and a cutting one from Aurora, who would gladly have disposed of the boy as she had designed in Harry's case, so that he would not trouble anyone in the future.

But Tom was not going to be what he called "cooled off," and, sitting down near Harry, he entered into a light and cheerful conversation, in which he was not so well supported as he deserved to be.

Unconscious that he had done anything more than spoil a "bit of spooning," he enjoyed the situation immensely, and played the part of an innocent interrupter to perfection.

"I started with Flowerpot," he said, "but the poor old chimpanzee caved in about half-way up. I left him a mile or so lower down singing an Abyssinian song for the dead. He thinks he is going to die."

"Was it kind of you to leave him?" said Harry. "Perhaps he is very ill. If I were you I should return to him without delay."

"If you were me," replied Tom, coolly, "you would do as I do. Flowerpot is a fraud. He can sham anything, and is the most consummate old scoundrel under the sun."

"What a name for the creature to have," said Aurora, with a curled lip.

Tom saw the expression of her face, but he did not mind what she thought. He was an embryo woman-hater, and took delight in quietly aggravating the sex generally.

"I named him," he answered proudly. "His real name is about four feet long, and nobody not in the know with the Abyssinian lingo can pronounce it, I call him Flowerpot because he is always blooming with something new. I say, what a jolly look-out we have here."

"The scenery is very fine," replied Harry, tartly.

"What it wants is a few tea-gardens scattered about it," said Tom, with a covert grin, "and some bowers for refreshment here and there would be useful and appreciated by some people. I say, are you going?"

Harry had risen, and in a vexed way he nodded assent.

Aurora asked him if he were going back to the hotel.

"I think so," he said, wearily, "unless you desire to prolong our stroll."

"It is my desire to return," she answered, "but it will be better for me to go alone."

"Alone?"

"I have said it," she answered. "I beseech you not to question what I do. It is my humour. Let that at present suffice."

She glided away with a quick step, and was well on the way down the path ere Harry broke the silence again. He was heartily vexed with Tom, but the innocent expression of the boy's face quite disarmed his anger.

"Tom," he said, "you were rather *mal apropos* just now."

"How is that ?" asked Tom.

"In the future, when you see two young people together—one of each sex, I mean—let them have their little talk out."

"Oh ! that's what is the matter."

Tom's surprise was overwhelming.

"I'll remember next time, but of course you could hardly expect me, young as I am, to know what's o'clock without being told."

A faint smile passed across Harry's face. With the departure of Aurora her influence seemed to be gone, and his vexation rapidly died away. He even reproached himself, as he journeyed down towards the hotel, with having allowed the magnetic power of the girl to wean him temporarily from the more serious work he had set himself to do.

And where was Wild Dick meantime ?

He started with the intention of keeping near his young master, for he was haunted with an indefinite idea that he was in peril. The erratic brain of the poor fellow was susceptible to all sorts of emotional currents, which carried him here and there as a straw is blown by the wind.

And ere he had reached the base of the mountain he met with a man strolling along leisurely through the valley, with a cigar in his mouth and a knapsack on his back.

He was a Frenchman, his name was Rigault, and he had the appearance of an ordinary tourist, which he certainly was not.

Wild Dick was a stranger to him, and he merely glanced at Dick as he passed by. Dick, on his part, looked keenly at the Frenchman, and then wheeled about and followed him.

The original purpose of the poor fellow was forgotten.

Rigault took his time in getting to the hotel, before which he paused with the air of a man who is uncertain whether he shall halt or not, and then in a leisurely manner he entered. Strolling to the clerk's office, he gave that important functionary the usual greeting.

Then he ordered something to drink, and looked over the visitors' book.

"Ah ! monsieur," he said, "you have many staying here."

"It is so," was the reply, "but one who was here yesterday has gone, and he will return no more."

In this way the clerk introduced the interesting theme of the murder of Hocknier. Rigault raised his eyebrows and looked curious.

"I don't think," continued the clerk, "he was a compatriot of yours, but a German, I believe. He was here, and he goes out this morning to be brought back with a bullet through his heart. Who put it there ? It is not for me to say, but behold a man of English breed, with a nose so red that the rose is pale beside it, flies away, and is not to be found. What then ? The mayor says it is he who has done the crime. Why ? Because there is a woman in the affair. Thus the mayor and the gendarmes, but it is not for me to say."

Rigault's eyebrows bristled, and he asked for a light, as his cigar had gone out. The clerk gave him one, and imparted the additional information that if monsieur would care to see the murdered man he could do so, for he was lying in the shed—the third on the right beyond the hotel—and the gendarme in charge would gladly exhibit the same for a franc. His pay being small, and having a large family, he was glad to add to his income by any honest means.

Rigault was travelling to see all things, he said, and therefore he would look at the dead man. But first another drink, and a strong one, for he was both thirsty and tired.

The drink was supplied him; he drank it off, and wandered out in a casual way to look at the dead man.

——— ———

CHAPTER XII.

WITHIN THE SHED—RIGAULT RECEIVES A WARNING AND FLIES—WILD DICK TELLS HIS MASTER SOMETHING—PURSUIT AND A SCENE BY THE RIVER.

OUTSIDE the first person Rigault saw was Wild Dick, squatted on the stone steps of the hotel. He recognised him as the man he had met in the valley, and once more those active eyebrows of his went up.

"Hey, there—you," he said, "have I not seen you before to-day?"

Wild Dick looked up at him with a vacant stare, but gave no reply. The porter of the hotel, who had followed Rigault out, took the trouble to explain to him who Dick was.

"He is a poor creature who follows his master like a dog," he said.

"And who is his master?" asked Rigault.

"He arrived but recently, and I know not," was the answer. "But there is no harm in this man; do not heed him, monsieur."

Rigault went on to the third hut beyond the hotel, where he found the gendarme keeping guard over the door, and in the complaisant mood of an exhibitor who hopes to turn an honest penny.

"Monsieur would like to see the murdered man, perhaps? It was not usual to exhibit such things, but—"

The sentence ended with the sight of the franc and Rigault was allowed to pass in.

It was an empty shed, save for a trestle and the dead. Hocknier lay there, with his hands crossed upon his breast, terribly white and still.

Rigault was not surprised, but the sight of his old companion was an undoubted shock to him. He stood by the rude bier, with the gendarme behind him, and for a minute or more did not stir.

"Ah, monsieur!" said the officer, "it is sad to see him—but yesterday alive and now *there*."

"It is horrible!" answered Rigault, drawing a long breath.

He was deeply affected, and the gendarme said it showed monsieur had a tender heart. Was it possible that monsieur, in his travels, had met him?

"I have never set eyes upon him before," replied Rigault, and with this lie upon his lips he turned and left the hut.

He returned to the hotel, and said he would stay there that day. Meanwhile, as he had some letters to write, he would be glad of a private room.

"Give me one in front—it is the warmer side of the place," he said.

They showed him into one, and supplied him with pen and ink; but instead of writing letters he sat down by the window, and from behind the curtain watched all that went on outside.

A few stragglers went in and out, but the majority of the visitors were on various excursions, so there was little to interest him until past noon, when he saw Aurora returning. She was alone, and walking quickly, as women do when troubled.

He stole out of the room and waited in the corridor until she came upstairs. They met, and, without a word, she motioned him to follow her to her own apartment.

It was that in which she had had an interview with Hocknier on the previous day. As soon as the door was closed she turned upon him.

"Why were you not here yesterday?" she demanded.

"I lost my way, coming on foot, and knowing not the country," he answered.

"It is the laggards who always breed trouble and thwart the purposes of their betters," she said. "Now, being here, depart again with all speed, unless you wish to lie beside Hocknier."

The colour fled from the face of Rigault.

"Then it was *he* who killed him?"

"No other," she replied; "and they have laid it to the charge of that bibulous fool because he has vanished. Why he should fly I know not, but he must be found and put out of the way. Hasten at once. Delay not a moment, or Harry Dalton may be here."

"He is but one," urged Rigault, "and I am one."

"I tell you that if you remain you are doomed. You do not know the man; he has been under-estimated by you all. Will you go?"

Her manner was as imperious as that of an empress, and, rising, Rigault bowed himself humbly out of the room.

Hastening downstairs, after having fetched his knapsack from the room he had engaged, he paid his bill and went on his way up the valley, occasionally casting apprehensive glances behind him.

One man marked the road he took, and that was Wild Dick, who from behind a sheltering rock kept his eyes upon him until he disappeared.

Barely had he vanished when Harry and young Tom were seen in the distance, and Wild Dick emerged from his hiding-place and hastened to meet him.

"Master," he said. "I have seen a foe to-day. He has a wolf's race and he talks French. He paid to see the dead man lying there ; after that he went to see *her*, and then he fled away."

Tom stared at the speaker, whom, in common with others, he looked upon as downright mad.

"Here is my purse," said Harry ; "pay the bill, Dick. Tom, you must convey my apologies to your father ; I am called unexpectedly away. One of these days we may meet again. Good-bye."

He shook hands with the boy, and was speeding down the valley before Tom could say farewell. Dick was already half-way to the inn.

"Well," said Tom, drawing a long breath, "I'll be hanged if this is not the champion licker of all I have seen for years. What does it mean? If that girl isn't at the bottom of it I'm a Hottentot. Anyway, she is left for me to keep an eye on her, and I'll do it. There is no fear of my getting spoons upon her, but the governor may, and I'll keep an eye on him too."

.   .   .   .   ,

Three days later, in the evening, two men were hiding in a small, out-of-the-way inn on the banks of the Rhine. They were Swivels and Rigault.

The Frenchman had tracked down the tutor with a surer instinct than the gendarmes had displayed, and come upon him in this lone place in an almost penniless condition. On both of them there was the fear of the man they knew to be in pursuit of them.

A telegram in cypher to Aurora had brought back a reply that left no doubt on that point. Translated, her answer was as follows—

On your track. Get on to Paris. There await instructions. The prince will be here to-morrow.

It was many miles to Paris, and the pair were going to travel warily by a devious route. As they sat in a back room Rigault was mapping it out.

"A boat will be ready in the morning by sunrise. By it we cross the river, and take the boat at Cravault. That will weaken the scent. He will never suspect our having gone there. Say a day or so for rest, and then on to Strasburg—from there to Paris and safety."

"I don't think that there is much safety for us anywhere," replied Swivels, miserably. "What is your league doing that you can't get the better of one man?"

"The league will settle one I know," said Rigault, savagely, "if he chatters too much. Hear me so far. Are we not scattered, idiot? Is not the hand of many nations against us, fool?"

"If you say so," answered Swivels, "it is so. I am not in your secrets, and why I should be mixed up in matters that don't concern me is what I cannot understand ; but do as you like."

It was growing dark then, but no light was brought, and they asked for none. To one at least it seemed as if there was no security in the gloom. Every noise outside brought them to their feet, and the sound of a voice set their hearts palpitating.

It was the death of Hocknier and the warning of Aurora that had brought them to this pass. As yet neither had seen any signs of Harry Dalton's coming, but both felt he was on their track.

"It is the work of a fool to be the tool of big men," said Rigault, after a pause. "The jackal finds the feast, and the monarch enjoys it. No sleep to-night, my friend—we shall start at dawn."

.   .   .   .

Dawn upon the Rhine is a beautiful hour. There is a freshness and a purity about it not found in many climes. The majestic surroundings, the rushing stream, the brilliant coming of the sun, all combine to give a rare charm to the scene. The poorest and meanest must each feel it to a degree.

Even Rigault, hardened villain as he was, did so as he stepped out from the inn to fly away to that region of safety, his beloved Paris.

Swivels had gone on before, and was already in the boat, impatiently awaiting his coming.

With a sense of relief he saw the Frenchman advancing, but it was quickly dispelled when from the open door of the inn another figure emerged and bore rapidly down upon him.

"Turn, Rigault, and meet your fate !"

The Frenchman pulled up dead, but he did not for the moment turn, because the power to do so was denied him. His very pulse stood still in the terror of the moment.

Swivels fell forward and lay prone upon the prow of the boat, a helpless, agonised spectator of the scene that ensued.

He saw Rigault, after a time, slowly wheel round and face the man he had learnt to dread. Some words, which the fear-stricken wretch in the boat could not grasp, were uttered by the pursuer, and then once more the Frenchman was flying towards the boat.

In vain was his attempt to get away."

"Will you not fight for your life ?"

These words rang out clearly enough, but the man to whom they were addressed only feebly responded to them.

He seemed to draw a weapon, as he turned again, rocking on his feet like a drunken man.

Then there was one report—or was it two ?—Swivels was not sure —and Rigault throwing up his arms fell heavily to the ground.

CHAPTER XIII.

TOM STARBUCK AND AURORA—ARRIVAL OF THE PRINCE—TOM
PLAYS THE SPY AGAINST HIS WILL.

MAJOR STARBUCK, on hearing of the departure of Harry Dalton, was inclined to be indignant ; but he was a man who, at the time, was living at ease, and he soon assuaged his wrath and pursued the even tenour of his way.

"I don't know why I should bother about him," he said to Tom, as they sat outside the hotel one evening ; "our acquaintance was of the most casual description. It was the fact of his being a Dalton that drew me towards him."

"He is not a bad sort of fellow," replied Tom, with a yawn, "but as soft with women as pap."

"What's that ?" demanded the major, sternly. "What do you know about being soft with women ?"

"I have eyes in my head," returned the unmoved Tom, complacently. "I say that he is clean gone on that girl whose name is Aurora Vaubertie. I don't think much of her myself."

The major glared at him with a true Roman father expression, but he might as well have thrown the angry glance away upon a woo den image. Tom did not notice it in the least.

"I've always observed," he went on, serenely, "that as soon as a fellow is gone on a girl he is fit for nothing but to make a fool of himself. He ought to be sent right away at once to some lone island and compelled to make a Robinson Crusoe of himself until he comes to his senses. Government ought to provide some place for the afflicted, just as they do penal settlements for criminals."

The major was smoking a big cigar, which he took from his mouth, the better to stare at his promising son. Tom, apparently unaware of being under close observation, remarked that it was a fine evening—a "regular girls' night," for moonlight was intended to make fools of the knock-kneed duffers who went wrong on them.

"Don't you think it is time for you to go to bed ?" suggested the major.

"I could not sleep a wink if I went," answered Tom. "But I think that a game of billiards would do you good. Don't mind me. I can spend an hour or so alone."

The major had long ago given up absolute control of his only son, and not being in fettle to pursue further conversation with him, he rose up and returned to the hotel.

A quiet grin spread itself over the face of the boy.

"I do like to stagger the governor," he murmured. "Now what shall I do with myself? Shall I take a stroll, or try to get some fun out of the people here? Hallo ! here is that girl, and, by Jove ! she is making for me. I fancied I made a bit of an impression upon her the other day. Tom, be firm. Don't be led away by the she-impostor."

Aurora had emerged from the hotel, and, after looking round and finding that the boy was outside alone, she came towards him, and sat down on the seat the major had vacated.

"It is fine to-night," she said.

"I suppose," replied Tom, "that you make that remark as a compliment to my nationality? All Britishers start a conversation with an allusion to the weather."

"You are a very original boy," said Aurora.

"Do you really think so?" rejoined Tom, "That is a real compliment, anyway."

"What has become of your friend?" asked Aurora.

"If you mean Dalton," answered Tom, "he is but a passing acquaintance, and I don't know."

"You won't know, you mean."

"Fact, I assure you," said Tom. "Come, now, do you for a moment believe that I would try and deceive *you?*"

"That is, I fancy, a compliment to me."

"If you like to take it that way. I do not think it would be easy to take you in. Dalton went away suddenly, and that is all I know about him."

Aurora bit her lip and stared at Tom, who, with a rather vacant expression, was surveying the moonlit landscape.

"I hope we shall be friends," she said, after a pause.

"I do not see why we should not make ourselves agreeable to each other," returned Tom. "I say, you must find it rather dull here alone."

"I expect my father, the prince, to-night," answered Aurora.

"Ah! he will be company for you."

"Not much, as he is always so busy. He is a diplomat."

The jingling of bells broke in upon the conversation, and they were both silent, with their eyes upon the valley from whence the sounds were heard.

From out the shadow of a huge rock a cavalcade of four persons upon mules advanced, and bore down upon the hotel.

The foremost rider was the prince, sitting his unruly beast like a cavalry officer, and occasionally striking it over the head with a stout stick he carried in his right hand. The men behind him had the appearance of followers, two of a high grade, and the third an unmistakable menial.

"This is the prince, I suppose?" said Tom.

"It is," replied Aurora.

"Then I will leave you," said Tom.

He rose up, bowed to her with the ceremonious grace of an old-time courtier, and sauntered into the hotel.

"On my word, she *is* pretty," he muttered. "Now, Tom, be firm. Do not forget the line you have chalked out for yourself. No spoons."

The majority of the guests were still at the table, lingering over their dessert. Tom looked in for a moment, helped himself to a bunch of grapes, and walked out again.

He did not see his father among the company, so he wandered

away to the billiard-room, where, standing at the door, he saw his parent engaged in a game with a German, who was not by any means a match for him.

"He is good for an hour," muttered Tom. "When the governor is on the winning lay he will go on until the other side cries, 'Hold, enough!' bless him."

With the grapes in his hand the boy sauntered upstairs and walked slowly down the corridor. At the far end was Aurora's room, and the door stood invitingly open.

Curiosity was one of Tom's weaknesses, and he could not resist the impulse to just have a look around the place. Accordingly he entered.

But barely had he done so when he heard footsteps and the voice of Aurora. A hot flush overspread his face, and he wished himself at Jericho.

Despite his indifference to the tender sex, he had a strong objection to their thinking meanly of him, and he would not have had Aurora think ill of him for a ten-pound note.

On one side of the room was a sofa couch, with a heavy valance to it. Acting on impulse prompted by mortification, he plunged underneath it, and lay as still as a mouse.

"I hope they are not coming in here," he groaned, "or, if they do, perhaps they will not stop long."

Coming in they were, and come in they did. Moreover, they sat down on the very sofa under which he was lying concealed.

Tom had not expected anything so serious as this, but, being in for whatever might happen, he screwed himself up to the sticking point.

"Now, Aurora!" said the prince, "I have heard something as I came along. Tell me exactly what has happened."

"Hocknier is dead," she said. "He was found shot. It was Harry Dalton's work."

"The luck goes with him as it went with his father years ago," said the prince, bitterly, "but our time will come again."

"Why not let the whole thing go?" asked Aurora.

"Impossible," answered the prince. "If even I were disposed to, which I am not, it could not be done. Our forces are scattered, or it would be ended in twenty-four hours."

"How goes it with us generally?" said Aurora. "Bad, I fear."

"Yes, bad," said the prince. "All the authorities are awake and stirring. There is red in the air for some of us. Who is at the hotel?"

"No spies," replied Aurora; "but there is a friend of Dalton's who would make a good pigeon if the plucking is done properly. He has a boy with him, a keen little fiend, who is apt to know more than is good for him."

"That IS a compliment," thought Tom. "Really, they have been flying thick to-day."

"What has become of Clewson?" asked Aurora.

"He is with me," replied the prince. "You did not recognise

him in his livery. It was necessary as a disguise, for he is wanted for some crime in his own country. Stork is with me also. He may be useful if there is rough work to do."

"He may wring the neck of that boy—the major's son," said Aurora. "But for the imp the whole of the work you have set your heart on would now be completed. By the way, I have not had a word from Rigault for twenty-four hours. It is hardly possible that he has fallen across Dalton."

A knock at the door interrupted them, and Aurora bade the new-comer enter.

It was Clewson, in a gorgeous livery of green and gold. He had a small tray in his hand, on which was the familiar telegram envelope.

"Just arrived," he said; "for you, Aurora."

Tom, who was taking a peep at the liveried Clewson from under he valance, was considerably astonished to hear him thus address the daughter of a prince.

He was still more dumbfounded when the apparent servant sat down.

"Let us have it," he said, bitterly. "Everything of late goes wrong."

"It is from Swivels," said Aurora. "Wait while I translate it."

The telegram was in cypher, and it took her several minutes to get at the meaning of it. She went through her task without betraying any emotion.

"Rigault was shot this morning by Dalton," she said, in a cold, hard voice, "and Swivels got away. He was carried down the Rhine in a boat, and picked up by a steamer. He was landed at Harlach, but not until the afternoon, or he would have wired before."

There was a silence after this, which was eventually broken by the prince.

"I mistrust your old tutor," he said. "If he dare betray us he would do so to-morrow."

"What is there for him to betray?" asked Clewson. "He knows nothing, nor do I. You have never trusted me fully."

"It was not necessary," was the cold reply.

"It will be necessary to trust me one day," said Clewson, "for the part of a blind tool is one I am tired of playing. I may as well risk my life in offending the league as in acting for the league."

"Save in this respect," said the prince. "By acting for the league you may escape death—by offending it your fate becomes a certainty."

"All this is idle talk," interposed Aurora. "What is to be done? Harry Dalton does not suspect me at present. Find out where he is gone, and I will throw myself in his way. I have him almost sure in the toils. The next time he shall not escape."

"Aurora," said the prince, "I have suspected you have been somewhat tender towards him."

"I sink all that," she answered. "Find him, I say, and I will lay aside all womanly softness. If I loved him as woman never loved before I would act for you. Do I come of a yielding stock? Have you ever swerved from your purpose of exterminating the race of Dalton? I think not. Now let us talk no more, but act. Clewson, you must trace him out. You are an adept at disguising yourself, and may escape his vengeful hand. Begone! We will away to Paris to-night."

"The old address, I suppose?" said Clewson.

"The same," answered Aurora.

There was a sound of moving feet, and Tom Starbuck, cautiously peeping under the valance, saw the door open and shut. Clewson was gone.

"Daughter," said the prince, as he embraced her, "forgive me. If I for a moment mistrusted you—"

"Say no more," she replied; "and now, as spies may be about, I mistrust that boy "—Tom shivered—"and we may be watched. Let us do as others do here to-day, and when night comes we will depart."

The pair left the room together, and Tom felt as if the weight of the Atlantic had been removed from his breast.

But, eager as he was to get away, he was too cautious to be in a hurry. He waited until he felt pretty certain the prince and his daughter were below ere he emerged from his hiding-place.

"I've got what I have wanted for years," he muttered, as he glided towards the door—"a really dangerous thing to do. I'll persuade pater to go to Paris, and I'll look out for Dalton and warn him against that girl. What a she-cat—what a female fiend! All right, Miss Pink-face; you may find me in the end a match for you."

He went off to his room, had a wash and brush-up, and ten minutes later was lounging about outside among the idlers, of whom the prince and his daughter formed a pair, with his hands in his pockets, as unconcerned as if he had heard nothing out of the common to trouble his youthful mind.

Aurora after a time beckoned Tom to her side, and was most gracious. She introduced him to her father, and later on the major had that honour also.

"We are going to Paris," said Aurora to Tom; "have you ever been there?"

"No," replied Tom, "but I should like very much to see the Queen City."

"Well, why not come with us?" suggested Aurora.

Tom appeared to hesitate, although here was the very thing he most desired. By falling in with her he could go to Paris without exciting suspicion.

"I'll ask pater," he said; "he generally gives way to me, but he is not fond of Paris. Perhaps, if you were to say a word for me, he might consent."

"I will do what I can for you," said Aurora, sweetly.

Tom was quite effusive in his gratitude, and the upshot of it was that the major consented to follow the prince and his daughter on the morrow, promising to call on them at their apartments—No. 16, Rue Riviera.

"I'm in for it now," thought Tom, as he got into bed that night. "It's a case of hit or miss—I settle them or they settle me. Can I trust pater? No, I think not. Alone, Tom, my boy, you must do the trick."

———

CHAPTER XIV.

AT PARIS—A LETTER AS A DECOY—THE LEAGUE AT HOME.

IT is a little world we live in, and sooner or later those whose lots are mingled come together after a severance, even though it be in a remote spot of the earth.

Harry Dalton, three weeks after the death of Rigault, found himself in Paris. He hardly knew why he went there, save that he was impelled to go, and Wild Dick, of course, went with him.

After the death of the Frenchman there was some anxiety on his part to know how the authorities would deal with the matter, but, as in the case of Hocknier, they blundered.

Once more Swivels got the credit of a deed he had not committed.

Who could suspect the young Englishman, who arrived at the old inn the night before, and paid his bill before he went to bed, saying that he was a tourist and would be gone with the sun in the morning?

So liberal a guest would have no hand in the tragedy that was afterwards discovered to have taken place on the banks of the river.

A dead man, and his friend in a boat missing. Only one interpretation could be put upon the affair, but the search after the supposed culprit was very lax, and ended when it was known that he had gone across the river and vanished.

Who was Rigault that there was any need for the authorities to excite themselves? Possibly some low adventurer or gambler, who had been quarrelling over the plunder of some innocent. It was not worth troubling about.

So to Paris Harry Dalton went, without any obstacles being thrown in the way, and there he put up at the Hotel Brussels, mooning about the Boulevards, doing nothing but expecting much.

Wild Dick, as he usually did, went his own way during the daytime. He was always looking for something he never found, but without disturbing his erratic mind; he was never lost.

No matter whither he wandered, he was sure, like a carrier-pigeon, to find his way home again.

Harry had been four days in Paris, and he was sitting outside a café in the Bois de Boulogne, when a man came up and put a small, scented envelope into his hand.

It was addressed to him in fine writing, of the polished aristocratic lady class, and he was not surprised on opening it to find that it came from Aurora.

He was not expecting anything of the sort from her, but he was not astonished, because he knew of no one else who would know his name or write to him.

The letter ran thus, without any pretext by way of address—

I saw you twice to-day, and you did not see me once. It is so easy for some to forget. Our home here is at 16, Rue Riviera and I am at home every Thursday.

AURORA VAUBERTIE.

He had not forgotten her, and he had not longed to see her. There was nothing in her letter really to lure him, and yet the moment he had read it he longed to see her.

"To-night is Wednesday," he murmured, "to-morrow is Thursday. It is not long to wait."

Life had been very dull to him of late. Wild Dick was no companion for him, aud he rarely conversed with strangers. It would at least be a change to call upon her. At an "At Home" there would be company, and he would find in the society of agreeable men and women what he had long sorely needed.

So he reasoned and went to his fate.

He wanted to kill the time until the morrow, and went to the Theatre Français. From a back seat in the dress-circle he scanned the house, and presently he saw her with no companion but a boy, whom he at first did not recognise.

But after a time he remembered the handsome, open face of the lad, and recalled his short acquaintance with Tom Starbuck.

The youngster seemed to be quite at home, and, with a lorgnette, scanned the house with the air of an *habitue*. Harry Dalton kept well back in the shade, as he did not wish to be recognised that night.

His first impulse was to go away, but he lingered until the last scene in the wonderful " Frou Frou "—the play for the night—and witnessed with a strange thrill the dying scene as performed by the incomparable actress.

There was no resemblance between her and Aurora, and yet it seemed as if there was some strong association between them.

The play over, he went into the lobby and watched until he saw Aurora ahead, going down the stairs to the lobby.

Tom Starbuck, as gallant a knight as ever the world has seen of his years, was in attendance upon her, but he only saw her to her carriage, and after a shake of the hand and a few laughing words from Aurora they parted, Tom sauntering off in his easy offhand manner.

It was a ridiculous feeling, but Harry Dalton could not help it. He was jealous of the boy, and he would not go after him and renew their acquaintance as he might otherwise have done.

The usual gaiety of Parisian life was around him, but Harry was in no humour to share in it. He was not faltering in the set purpose of his life—to avenge the death of his father and brother—but he was conscious of a weakening somewhere. He drifted into Paris, and was floating about like a straw on the turbid lake of living men and women, until that night.

Now he was going to see Aurora again, drawn towards her, yet repelled, eddying in his thoughts, but ever bearing to the centre of the maëlstrom.

At the corner of the Bois de Boulogne a crowd had gathered.

There were loud talkers in English and French, the former very rough amidst the authoritative tones of the ubiquitous gendarme.

It was something to hear and see, and Harry stopped on the outskirts of the mob.

Immediately afterwards the circle of gazers was rent in twain, and two men came through the opening struggling together.

One was a gendarme, and the other was the ruffian Stork. They were grappling together, and the latter had the French officer by the throat, holding him with the tenacity of a bull dog.

"I'll not be taken!" he yelled. "What have I done? He kicked at me. Do you call that a fair fight, you mongrels? I've nigh twisted his leg off, as any other man would have done."

A second gendarme broke through the crowd and came to the aid of his fellow-officer. They all three fell together, and the wild mob capered and screamed around them like evil spirits in Hades.

Stork fought with the strength of a giant and the courage of a lion. Whatever he may have been in character, he did not lack pluck.

Harry had marked the fellow for one of his victims, but he could not help sympathising with him against the odds he had to contend with.

Stork struck one of his would-be captors with his clenched fist upon the temple, and, wrenching himself from the others, jumped to his feet. For a moment or two he stood glaring at the howling mob, all of whom shrank back from his fierce looks and threatening air.

As he wheeled round in search of a fresh foe to conquer his eyes fell upon Harry Dalton, and his brute courage instantly evaporated.

"Don't shoot!" he cried, throwing up his hands.

"I am not going to hurt you," answered Harry. "Why don't you get away, man? If they run you into prison you will be sent to the gallows for this."

"You're right," muttered Stork.

Plunging into the thick of the vehicular traffic in the road he disappeared.

The two gendarmes got up slowly, staring about them like the half-dazed men they were. The crowd at once began to laugh and jeer them.

"Too much little John Bulldog pig," said a woman, with a flaunting air. "See, there is another of the breed; take him."

She pointed to Harry Dalton, who paid no heed to her, but the gendarmes, for the lack of another victim, bade him roughly begone.

He did not stir, and they pushed him unceremoniously. The rag-tag and bobtail around hilariously hailed it as a good joke.

"What is it you want?" demanded Harry. "Is it your intention to escort me to your superiors? If so, let it be done at once."

They seemed disposed to take him at his word, but ere they could act a man of high bearing and haughty demeanour thrust them aside.

"You dogs!" he said. "Is there to be no end to your jackanape authority?"

It was the Prince Vaubertie, and he was evidently known to the gendarmes, for they shrank back, and the prince, taking Harry's arm, led him away.

"How is it," he asked, "that you became mixed up in a vulgar street brawl? It is not your nature to quarrel with anyone."

"It was really not my affair," replied Harry. "But pardon me, prince, while I am grateful to you for your interference, there is a matter between us that requires some explanation."

The prince raised his eyebrows and looked puzzled.

"Do you remember that night at Calais?" asked Harry.

"I remember many nights, my young friend," replied the prince. "I am often there."

"I am alluding to the night when we crossed the Channel together," pursued Harry.

"That night?" said the prince, with a meditative air; "I cannot recall it. Oh! yes, I remember. I left the boat and came straight into Paris. I did not stay there at all."

"And yet I saw somebody like you," insisted Harry; "so like that I would have sworn it was you."

"I was not there," replied the prince, emphatically; "but now you name it I call to mind my cousin Lucien was there."

"Are you alike?"

"So much so that we are often mistaken for each other. But we seldom meet; his ways are not my ways—his people not my people. He is no credit to our family."

The air, the manner of the prince, was convincing. Harry felt assured that he had made a mistake; but how could he explain?

It was not possible for him to tell the prince that he suspected him of being leagued with assassins.

All he could do was to turn the subject by saying that he was mistaken, and the prince condescendingly let the matter slide.

"By the way, my young friend," he said, "what are you doing with yourself to-night?"

"I am thinking of going to rest," answered Harry.

"Pshaw, to rest at midnight and guard the flower of youth?"

said the prince. "It is not to be thought of. I am not going to retire myself. Come, let me show you a little life. It will please you—rouse you—for I see you are hipped. Here is a place, now, that will amuse you."

He stopped in the front of a house that was all dark, and not by any means inviting in any sense. Harry hesitated, and the former laughed merrily.

"No outside show," he said, "but all so bright within. You play? No? Then look on; it is enough. Come and see me make a fool of myself. Nay, you shall."

He held Harry by the arm, and, with a dexterous twist, got him through the outer door, which swung upon its hinges.

Inside all was dark as pitch.

"Stand!" said a voice, a few feet away.

The speaker was not visible.

"It is I," answered the Prince Vaubertie, "with a friend—a recruit."

Harry held back, and would have gone forth again, not being satisfied with his surroundings, but several hands were laid upon him, and he was propelled onward.

"Be not alarmed," said the prince, cheerily. "This is one of our little jokes."

"I have an Englishman's obtuseness," replied Harry, sternly, "and fail to see the joke."

"It will be as clear as noonday to you anon," was the rejoinder.

A bell was now heard to tinkle, and a door was thrown open, revealing a room of forbidding appearance, faintly lighted by two candles on a deal table in the centre of the room.

Around it were gathered a dozen men or more. They seemed to be of all classes, from the aristocrat to the peasant, judging by their dress. At the head of a table sat a man of majestic bearing, but with a mask covering his face.

"Take it as it is meant—for a jest," whispered the prince in Harry's ear. "We are a merry lot of fellows, as you will presently see."

"I will not be jested with," cried Harry. "Hands off, or I fight."

––––––––

CHAPTER XV.

THE FIGHT IN THE GAMBLING-HOUSE—HARRY GIVES A GOOD ACCOUNT OF HIMSELF—THE SECRET WAYS OF THE DEN.

THOUGH outnumbering Harry by a dozen to one, the men in the room looked at him with a doubtful eye, and several drew back, as if they feared him.

It might be that his reputation as a shot had gone before him, but, whatever may have been the feelings that inspired them, it is certain they exhibited a lamentable lack of courage.

The prince gazed at them with an ugly frown upon his brow, but when he again turned to Harry Dalton he had resumed his smile.

"It is natural to you English," he said, "to assume a trouble and then brace yourself to meet it like men."

"With your permission, prince," replied Harry, firmly, "I would rather not remain here. I have no taste for gambling in any shape or form, and I do not care for my present company—always excepting yours, of course."

"Do as you please," answered the prince, with an assumption of calmness. "I thought life in Paris was dull for you, not having any friends, and I only desired to break the monotony of it."

He turned away with an offended air, and Harry for the moment felt sorry. After all, he might have made a mistake in the character of the man.

Moreover, it flashed upon him that his fears might be unworthy of him. Nobody as yet had offered to attack or injure him in any way.

"Prince," he said, "if you intend to gamble for awhile, I will remain and look on. If I have unintentionally offered an insult to any of these *gentlemen* I beg to offer them an apology."

"Well said," returned the prince, with an appearance of frankness. "I am sure that none here will think the worse of you for having shown a manly independence of spirit. What say you, my friends?"

"Monsieur has only excited our admiration," replied a swarthy-faced man who was trifling with a pack of cards, apparently to while away the time.

Harry walked to the table and sat down.

"Go on with your play," he said.

Although he had, to all appearance, discovered that he had made a mistake, he was not at all reassured as to the character of the company he was in. On the contrary, he was more certain than ever that they were a dangerous lot of men.

Moreover, he was convinced that the prince was, as he suspected long before, an enemy of his, and was in reality responsible for the dark tragedy which had wrecked his home.

But ere proceeding against them he must be well assured that it was so, and he must also know the secret source of inspiration that led up to that calamity.

At present he had no clue whatever, and the only man outside the secret league against him who could furnish the information was Wild Dick, and he was not in a condition to do so, owing to his mental state.

The players drew up to the board and sat down, leaving Harry, to all appearance, a free agent. He sat in such a position that he could face them all, and he thrust his hands seemingly carelessly into his pockets, grasping, so as to be ready for immediate action, the brace of revolvers by means of which he held the lives of twelve men in his hands.

The swarthy man was banker, and the game was the notorious

baccarat. He dealt out the usual number of cards, beginning with the prince, who presently said—

"I take cards."

A few were dealt to him until he held up his hand. Then the dealer went on to the next, and so on right through them all.

Some took cards and some did not, and all seemed to be very intent on the play. The dealer took two for himself and threw his hand upon the table.

"I pay on eleven," he said.

About two-thirds claimed to be winners, and while he was paying them he suddenly stopped and challenged one man's stakes.

"You had one louis just now," he said. "How shall it be that you at this moment have two?"

"You lie!" was the angry retort; "I had two down from the first."

"I appeal to all here," said the dealer. "Was it so?"

"It was so," replied the prince.

Another said it was not so, and the opinion of the players varied so that the sides on the question were pretty equally divided.

Harry watched the wrangling that ensued with a curious eye. It was a proof to him that the life of a gambler were both exciting and quarrelsome.

Warmer and warmer waxed the dispute, until the man charged with cheating suddenly sprang up and fired a revolver at the banker.

The shot was ill-aimed, probably intentionally so, and smashed a looking-glass behind him. In prompt response all were immediately on their feet, and weapons were freely drawn.

The prince alone was comparatively quiet, and on him Harry kept a close watch.

He soon doubted the whole thing as a genuine fight, with too good a cause, as events proved.

Suddenly, as it appeared to him, several weapons were turned towards himself, and then he thought it was time for him to act.

Springing to his feet, he produced his revolvers, and covered two men nearest to him.

"I am going," he said, "and let none here attempt to stop me."

Two shots whistled by his head, and then, feeling certain that the whole thing was a fraud, and got up for the purpose of shooting him down, he began to fire.

The men he had covered fell, and then there was an undisguised attack upon him.

The prince, laying aside his coolness, called upon the remaining men to attack him, and, sinking their sham dispute, they directed their weapons towards Harry, who emptied six of the chambers of his revolvers so rapidly that the repeating shots sounded like a small fusilade. For every shot a man fell, and the floor was strewn with the still forms of those who died under his unerring aim.

At the same time he backed quickly to the door, and threw his whole weight against it.   With a crash it was burst from its hinges, and dropped on the floor of the passage.

The curses of the remaining gamblers were horrible to hear, and they for the most part took refuge under the table, or behind pieces of furniture that offered them temporary safety.

Again was the prince the director of their movements, for he stood up boldly with a face distorted with wrath, calling hoarsely on his confederates not to let "the accursed Dalton go."

"You dog and traitor," cried Harry, "I spare you now, but your hour will come."

"Kill him !" screamed the prince.

But Harry had already retreated down the passage on his way to the outer door.

There he expected to find a further obstacle in his way, but there was not.   The very fastenings had not been secured, and by merely turning the handle he found himself in the street.

The next moment every light in the house went out.

Not caring to linger in such a dangerous place, he walked quickly away until he came to a populous thoroughfare, where he hailed a passing vehicle, and bade the driver take him to his hotel.

It was very late, and the streets were rapidly thinning, but the hotel was still open, and he found Wild Dick on the steps awaiting his return.

"Master," he said, "where have you been ?   I have had ugly dreams of you to-night."

It was a way of Dick to call his thoughts "dreams," and his troubled face showed that he had been worried with apprehensive thoughts concerning his master.

"I have been where none but a fool would have gone," answered Harry.   "I will not talk of it to-night.   It is time you and I were asleep."

He had a room on the first floor, to which he swiftly ascended Dick followed him to the door, but he waved him away.

"Not now, Dick," he said ;   "to-morrow."

Then he went in and closed the door, but Wild Dick did not go to his own chamber, which, in common with that of the other servants, was high up in the roof.

He lingered about the well-lighted corridor muttering to himself, and when any of the servants came along he feigned to be moving away, but he always returned to his post.

When at last the outer door of the hotel was closed, and all but the night watchman retired, he was still there, and lay down on the mat like a faithful dog.

"Here I rest," he murmured.   "I must be near him.   The place is thick with his enemies, but who would have his life must first take mine."

CHAPTER XVI.

THE FOILED GAMBLERS—AURORA THROWS UP HER TASK—THE CHOSEN ASSASSIN.

WHEN the lights of the gambling house were extinguished the survivors of the defeated band left the house by a back way. Scattering, so as not to excite attention, they made their way separately to the house occupied by the prince in the Rue Riviera.

There was nothing to excite attention about it, for as far as the outside went it might have been nothing more than the modest home of a moderately successful merchant.

The prince was the very first to put in an appearance there, and he let himself in with a key. In the hall a small lamp was burning on a table, and there were two or three letters and telegram awaiting him.

The prince glanced quickly at their contents, and none of them appeared to be of a pleasing nature, as he bit his lip and uttered an angry exclamation more than once as he perused them.

"The luck goes against us everywhere," he said. "Is the breaking-up at hand?"

He had left the door ajar, and taking up the lamp, he walked up the thickly-carpeted stairs.

Though the exterior of the house was plain, the interior was most profusely decorated, and the furniture of the richest description.

As he reached the corridor above a door opened, and Aurora came forth. She was clad in a plain white garment of some warm, soft material, which hung loosely about her.

In appearance she rivalled in beauty the Greek statues that men are wont to rave about.

Her face was very pale, and there was a sad yet determined look in her eyes.

"Where have you been?" she asked.

"To Parleaux's den," he answered.

"Not to gamble, surely?" she said. "That was the vice of your youth. It is time for you to think of your advancing years."

"I am a man in my prime," replied the prince, "and, as such, think not of the flight of time."

"What has happened?" she inquired, looking closely at him. "Something has gone wrong."

"Are all the servants abed?"

"These two hours."

"It is well; I have a few friends coming. Hark! I hear one of them below."

"They know their way," said Aurora, with a bitter emphasis. "Your friends, both rich and poor, make free of your house. Come here with me."

She led him somewhat unwillingly into the room she had just vacated. It was her own room, furnished with great taste and elegance. Velvet lounges were disposed around, also quaint tables adorned with flowers, and beautiful pictures and china decorated the walls.

The prince threw himself down upon a lounge, and, resting an arm upon the back of it, looked his daughter in the face.

"I would tell you a lie," he said, "if I thought it were possible to deceive you, but it is not. By chance I met Dalton to-night. There was a row in the street with that fellow Stork, who likes nothing so well as a coarse fight. Dalton was near the crowd, and I spoke to him."

"Well ?"

"It is not well, but ill. I thought it would be a good opportunity to dispose of him for good and all, so I lured him into Parleaux's den, and gave the sign that he was to be settled."

"And is it done ?"

"No. If it were, should I look as I do to-night ? The man is a tiger, a fearless wretch, with the eye of an hawk and the steady hand of a machine. A quarrel was got up, and he was in the thick of a fire intended for him alone ; but he bore a charmed life, which none of the crew did. He left a little host of dead behind him."

"So he got away," said Aurora, with a brightening face. "Oh ! what a fool you were. He will not come to me now."

"And you seem glad."

"I rejoice at it, for this night I renounce the league. I would have done it to-morrow, and warned him."

"Aurora, do you know what you are saying ? Is not this one of your changeable humours ?"

"No, I know the risk I run. I am prepared to meet it. Would you have your daughter fear death ? Slay me if you will, for I am tired of my life."

The prince looked at her with imperfectly concealed dismay. He could see that it was no thought of the moment, no passing expression of weakness, but a stern resolve, and his heart sank within him.

"Aurora," he said, with a quavering in his voice, "you must do as you please. Go to him now. He is at the Hotel Brussels. Awake him, and say your father is—what he is. Offer to betray the secrets of us all. I will not stop you."

"I can do nothing now, nor will I attempt it," he answered. "Were I to do so he would not believe me. He knows you, and therefore knows me. I go to-night to begin a new existence—to expiate my sins in a life of poverty. As yet these hands of mine are free from blood. It is not your fault, however, that I have not a murder on my soul. All your teachings have been evil ; the good has never been shown to me. I go to seek it among strangers."

"You will not live to find it," said the prince, ominously. "Remember that no traitor is spared, and none are so traitorous as those of our own flesh and blood who betray us. Hear me for a moment. Let me tell the story of the wrong the father of this young Dalton did me."

"Your friends will grow tired of waiting," she said, coldly.

"Let them wait," he answered.

"Not so," she rejoined. "I have no desire to hear the story, unless it goes to show that Harry Dalton has wronged you."

"Personally he has not."

"Then why seek his life?"

"Because he is a Dalton."

"It is not enough," said Aurora. "As well blame him for having been born. But you are a fool, wise as you are deemed by some to be. Can you not see that all our efforts to destroy him will be *nil*. Are you so blind that you cannot see the handwriting on the wall, which tells you plainly that if you do not turn from your evil ways you are doomed?"

"Away with you, faint heart. You are not of our house," said the prince, wrathfully.

"I would I were not," she said, with a moan, "tossed about with your teachings and the pleadings of my own heart. I tell you, father, that in spite of all I have done for you to lure Harry Dalton to his fate I LOVE him. Not that it matters now, as I would never willingly see him more. I go away to-night to a new life. If you think it needful to put an end to me, seek me out and do your will."

He made a movement towards her, but she drew a dagger from her breast and stood firmly before him.

"Advance another step," she said, "and I will spare you a crime by taking my own life. Stand back."

He dropped upon the couch again, and sat there with bent head, shaking with emotion from head to foot.

Here, before him, was the only living thing he loved.

Aurora occupied the one green spot in his withered heart, and he had not dreamt of such a time as this. It tried him sorely, bitterly. Swiftly he ran over the past.

Why not have reared her as the daughters of other men—in simplicity and in truth? Was it too late to set her free and hold her by more worthy ties?

So he went on softening, and when at last he resolved to screen her by every means in his power from the penalty of turning from the league, and even to sacrifice himself for her sake, he lifted up his head to declare as much, and found that she was gone.

With a sickening feeling at his heart he rose up and left the room, and looked about the corridor for her in vain.

There was a murmuring of voices in a chamber on the other side, and, crossing to the room, he opened the door and entered.

The remnant of the gamblers were there, impatiently awaiting his coming. Once more his mind was steel, and in response to the frowns upon their faces he walked to the head of the table and struck it angrily with his hand.

"What is the meaning of these ugly looks?" he demanded.

"Am I your slave, that I am to be taken to task for a trifling mishap?"

"So many slain," said the swarthy-faced banker, who was one of the survivors, "is not a trifle. My brother Pierre is among the dead."

"Your brother Pierre," returned the prince, coolly, "should have learnt to shoot straight. Am I to blame for his faulty training? All of you take example from the young Englishman in the way you use your weapons. But forgive me ; it is not a subject for jest. The death of our comrades must be avenged. Harry Dalton sleeps at the Hotel Brussels. The night watchman is one of us. He will admit you, show you to his room, and on the morrow be as ignorant as you will of what is done. Who volunteers for the honour of slaying the man who has killed so many good men to-night?"

There was no immediate response. The task did not appear to commend itself to any of them.

"It must be a matter of luck, then," said the prince. "Gascoigne, get me a pack of cards from the cabinet."

Gascoigne was the swarthy-faced man. He did as he was told, and threw a pack of cards upon the table, face downwards.

"Each choose a card," said the prince, "and he who draws the lowest has the honour of the killing of our foe."

The men, with assumed nonchalance, drew a card and turned it over. All but Gascoigne and another had high cards. The two latter-named had each drawn a deuce, and therefore had to draw again.

Gascoigne allowed the other to select a card first, and as he exhibited a three of hearts Gascoigne smiled.

"It is yours," he said.

Then he drew his second card, and it was another deuce.

"It is for you to do it," said the prince, quietly. "Away at once, or the night will be gone."

Gascoigne was very pale, but he had nothing to say, and with an assumption of coolness left the room.

"Messieurs," said the prince, "we will now part. You will have notice of our next meeting."

He favoured them with a general bow, which they returned, and rising from their seats departed in silence.

The moment they were gone the whole aspect of the prince changed, and bowing his head upon the table he gave way to the bitterest reflections.

.   .   .   '   .   .   .   .   .   .

The hall-porter of the Hotel Brussels was dozing in his chair when a short, sharp rap was heard on the door. He was awake and on the alert in an instant.

If it had been one of the guests demanding admittance he would have rung the night-bell. Too well the porter knew that the late comer was of a different mould to the ordinary frequenters of the place.

For a moment he sat still, then, drawing a deep breath, he rose up and walked to the door, on which he knocked twice by way of reply.

In response there were three more knocks, and then he opened the door.

Gascoigne came with a noiseless footstep, for he had what are known as "silent boots" upon his feet, the soles being made of indiarubber. The porter closed the door again, and with a white face turned towards his visitor.

"What is the call?" he asked. "It would be ruin for me to leave my post to-night."

"You can remain," answered Gascoigne, "for, see, my work is here."

He brought out from under his coat a short, heavy life-preserver, at the sight of which the porter shivered.

"It is better than the knife or the pistol," Gascoigne said. "One makes a noise and the other leaves a stain. Where is the young Englishman sleeping?"

"What has he done?" asked the porter.

"It is not for you to know," was the reply. "Come, time presses. I must begone from Paris in an hour."

"If it is commanded, it must be done," said the porter, "but if I had not a wife and child I would say it should not be."

"You speak treason," responded Gascoigne, sternly.

"Charge me with it and I will say you lie," answered the porter, coolly. "You will find him in the third room on the right from the top of the stairs, first flight."

"Is there a light above?"

"No."

"How is the bed placed?"

"Opposite the door."

"Which he has locked, perchance."

"The lock is out of order and there is no bolt."

Gascoigne gave a nod of satisfaction and went softly on his way. The porter resumed his seat in the chair and sat there white and still and listening.

Up the stairs, with no more sound than a cat would have made, went the chosen murderer, step by step, with his big ears on the stretch to catch the slightest sound. Above all was still.

He reached the landing and found it very dark. Two heavy curtains had been drawn across the corridor to deaden the sound, so that the sleepers might not be disturbed. Cautiously the ruffian felt his way to the first door, and from thence along the wall until he reached the third one, and there he stumbled over the form of the faithful servant of Harry Dalton.

It was a complete surprise to him, and a startled exclamation burst from his lips.

The next moment he was grappling with Wild Dick, and at a venture he struck out fiercely with the life-preserver.

A dull thud followed, and it was succeeded by a scream so shrill and terrible to the ear that it aroused a score of minor echoes in the vast building. Sleepers awoke, and, tumbling from their beds, rang the bells, muttering cries of alarm.

As if by magic the whole place seemed to be awakened.

Men and women emerged from their rooms, some with lighted lamps or candles in their hands, and among them was Harry Dalton, who saw Wild Dick still holding on to Gascoigne, both on the floor.

From above a number of officials of the hotel, with the manager half-dressed to the fore, came pouring down, and in a thrice the dismayed Gascoigne was secured.

The hall-porter had perforce to appear on the scene, and he came tottering up the stairs to see what had caused the failure of the midnight attempt upon the life of the English guest.

Gascoigne was standing like a sullen beast in the toils, held fast by half a dozen men. Around him were the guests who had emerged from their rooms, and Harry Dalton was holding the insensible form of Wild Dick in his arms.

"Say, now," cried the manager, addressing the porter, "how came this man in the establishment ?"

"I know not," replied the porter. "I have not seen him in my life before."

Gascoigne did not look at him, or make a sign or say a word. He simply stood still, dumb, and apparently indifferent to whatever they might assume against him.

"Summon the gendarme," said the manager. "Again I ask the question," he continued, turning to Harry. "This man," pointing to Wild Dick, "is your servant. Is it not so ?"

"He is," answered Harry.

"Speak, then. How comes it that he is about the hotel at this hour ?"

"He is a good servant, with peculiar notions of duty. I judge that he was sleeping by my door to-night, and thus encountered this man, of whom I know something."

Gascoigne awoke from his stolid condition, and turning fiercely upon Harry, said—

"You lie ! Until this moment I never set these eyes of mine upon you."

"And I say," retorted Harry, "that *you* lie. You were one of those brutes who, in a gambling hell, attempted to take my life a few hours ago."

"Say, then," said the manager, "where shall that be ?"

"I do not know the name of the street," answered Harry, "for I am almost a stranger in Paris, but I have spoken the truth all the same."

Gascoigne smiled, with an effort to appear contemptuous.

"It is enough," he said. "There is no hell for gambling, and I know you not. Behold, I come here to-night, no matter how. Say that I am here for a long time hiding, and I come out to rob a little. I do not deny it. See him there—he who is so still from the blow I gave him ? He is lying there by the door, and I stumble over him. We have some fight in the dark, and I strike him to get away. It is all. He was rough with me. That is the whole story, and for me there is a little of prison—no more. I defy you all. Poof !"

Two gendarmes now appeared, accompanied by the hall-porter, who hung discreetly in the rear. They took possession of Gascoigne, securing his hands and listening to the manager's version of the affair.

He had no more to say than what Gascoigne had told him, and the officers took the matter coolly. Meanwhile Harry carried Wild Dick into the room, and despatched one of the servants for a physician.

The excitement was almost over, and the aroused guests and some of the servants returned to their rooms. The manager, having seen the prisoner taken away, and given an undertaking to appear before the prefect of police early on the morrow, came back to the chamber where the injured man was lying.

"It is a pity," he said, "so fine and faithful a man. How much better for him to have slept and the little robbery be done."

"I have good reason to know," answered Harry, quietly, "that more than robbery was intended. It was my life which was to be taken, and I owe it to this poor fellow here, for I was sleeping soundly at the time."

"I do not understand," said the manager, with a puzzled face. "How is it ? Why should he of the gambling hell come to kill you ?"

"It is a matter I cannot fully explain here," said Harry. "For the present let it rest."

"Ah !" exclaimed the manager, in the tone of a man who does not clearly understand or entirely believe a story.

Wild Dick gave no sign of returning life, and lay motionless until the physician arrived. He was a grave, elderly man, with a thick crop of white hair cut close to his head. His face was clean shaven, and it was of the mould which shows more than ordinary intelligence. His eyes were large, dark, and expressive.

Quietly and methodically he examined the patient, and discovered that he had received a blow upon the head, which, owing to Wild Dick's long hair, had not broken the skin.

"And yet it has injured the bone," he said, thoughtfully. "The blow was a terrible one. Nay, more, he has been struck on the same place before, but it was long ago."

"How do you know that ?" asked Harry, in surprise.

"Look at this," said the physician, and with a pair of small pocket scissors he rapidly cut away the hair from the injured place. "Mark the indentation that is old and that which is new. Almost the same spot. It is strange—it is marvellous. The case is interesting."

"You are right about his having been struck before," said Harry, "and he has had a weak, wandering mind ever since. I fear now he will die."

The physician did not immediately reply. He stood with his eyes on the recumbent form of Dick with the air of one who is working out a mental problem.

"Die—die," he said at last, "perhaps, but it may not be. I have longed for such a case as this. Say that I operate on him. Well, he may die, but if he shall live then his lost mind will be restored."

"Will he die if he is not operated on?" asked Harry.

"Most surely," was the reply.

"Then do as you will with him," said Harry, "and it is my earnest hope for his sake and mine that you may be successful in giving him back his life and reason. Your fee shall be a liberal one."

"It is not a question of fee," answered the physician, "but great fame for me. To-morrow, with the daylight, I will make my grand experiment. To-night he will not harm, and I must return to sleep for awhile, as I shall have need of a clear brain and a steady hand."

CHAPTER XVII.

WORK OF THE PHYSICIAN — A TIME OF ANXIETY — THE AWAKENING.

AT length the morning came, and at an early hour a young fellow arrived and introduced himself to Harry Dalton as the assistant of Dr. Leclerc, who would soon arrive to perform the operation on the still unconscious Dick.

The new arrival brought with him a case of instruments, which he opened and proceeded to lay out beside the bed, upon a table, with loving care.

Harry Dalton was not of a very nervous nature, but the sight of the keen-edged little weapons of the surgeon's art sent a thrill through him.

"These must be made of good metal," he said.

"They are of the finest steel," replied the assistant, "as good and better than the metal of which the ancient and much-boasted-of Toledo blades were made. If they were not pliable and strong at the same time our work could not be performed."

"Will the operation be a painful one?" asked Harry.

"I believe so," was the reply, "but look at the results."

"If successful."

"Just so."

Leaving him to his preliminary work, Harry Dalton went into the corridor, and walked up and down until the physician arrived. He came up the stairs slowly, with a thoughtful face, and saluted Harry courteously.

"It will be better for you to be in the room," he said, "to be a witness of the operation. In case of failure it is desirable. I must be frank with you—the slightest false movement will be fatal."

"He must die, poor fellow, unless the operation is performed," replied Harry, calmly. "Let us get it over as soon as possible."

"We cannot hasten anything," said the physician. "Every step must be taken with caution."

All was ready in the room, down to the basin of water and an arrangement of towels. Wild Dick had been propped up in the bed, ready for the chief actor in the drama.

He pulled off his coat, bared his arms, and selecting a narrow saw, about five inches long, motioned to his assistant that he was to stand aside.

To the imagination of those who love ghastly details we must leave the rest of the dreadful next half-hour.

Grain by grain, as it were, the skilled, cool operator felt his way. The bone that had so long been pressing on the brain of poor Dick was cut away and lifted up, to be again replaced with a thin silver sheet, or rather rim, by way of support.

The whole was fixed with a careful, steady hand, with now and then a fearful shriek from the patient, which went through Harry like a knife.

At length the physician turned to Harry with the light of triumph on his face, and in a low yet exultant voice said—

"It is done."

"And he will live?" said Harry.

"With care, but perfect quiet is essential. He must not be mentally or physically disturbed, say, for the next three days. After that you may talk to him freely. Leave him to come out of the darkness of so many years *alone*. He will find his way back."

Harry grasped the hand of the physician and thanked him with all his heart. The assistant, too, had his share of commendation.

But neither seemed to think so much of the patient as the fact that a novel operation had been successfully performed.

"I have two witnesses," said the physician, as he resumed his coat; "to-morrow I will get my article written and translated into English, German, and Russian, so as to appear simultaneously in all countries, or some charlatan will propound the thing as his own discovery."

He once more refused to take a fee, and departed, but his assistant remained to watch over the patient, who was now calmly sleeping.

"It will be better for you now to see nothing of him until he is fully restored," said the assistant. "He will not remember you as he has known you in his weakness."

"Is it possible?" exclaimed Harry.

"His mind will go back to the very hour when he lost his wits," said the assistant—"that is, from thence he will start afresh. All the rest will be a blank."

"Absolutely?"

"I should say so."

If that were indeed to be the case the situation was a peculiar one.

Harry would be a complete stranger to the man who, in his wild way, had served him well and been so faithful to him. What would be the future relation between them?

The more Harry thought of it the more he was puzzled. Would it be for good or ill, this coming back to the reason lost so many years ago?

The day passed, and Dick slept on. Late in the afternoon the attendant announced to Harry that he was awake.

"And how is it with him?" asked Harry.

"He is lying still, thinking like a puzzled child," was the answer.

Later on, as it was growing dark, Dr. Leclerc came back to see how the patient was progressing. The multifarious duties of his life prevented his doing so before. Harry, keeping out of sight in the shadow of the lower curtains of the bed, listened to the few words that passed between them.

"You are better," said the doctor, calmly.

"I am, sir," replied Dick, in a low tone. "Have I been ill for long?"

"For many days."

"Was it fever, sir?"

"Yes, and a very bad one; but you must not talk or worry yourself with thinking. All you have to do is to keep very quiet."

"But you can tell me one thing," said Dick. "Is master here, sir?"

"No, but you will see him when he returns. I must talk to you no more. Obey all instructions, and keep quiet."

The physician drew the curtains close, and Harry stole outside the room. Doctor Leclerc followed him.

"He asked for me," said Harry.

"Not for you," replied the doctor, "but for the master of the old times."

"What a shock it will be for him when he learns that he is dead."

"He must not receive it until he is strong enough to bear it. Ere he sees you he must be gradually led up to expect great changes, and the knowledge of the length of his illness imparted to him by degrees."

We must pass over the next few days, during which the most unremitting care was given to the patient by the doctor, his assistant, and a change of skilled nurses. Harry, acting on the advice first given, kept out of sight.

At last the hour came when Doctor Leclerc thought that an interview might be risked, and he proposed to stay in the room and see the effect of it.

It was in the evening, and the stronger light of day was on the wane, when Harry went in and sat down by the bedside.

Master and man looked at each other, both wonderingly.

Dick was no longer the wild-eyed, tawny man he had been, but a quiet-looking fellow of the upper servant type, who had the appearance of just recovering from a long illness.

Harry bore a strong resemblance to what his father had been in the old time as far as face and form went, but in dress and bearing there was a wide divergence.

"I am glad to see you, sir," said Dick, in a slow way, "but I don't seem to quite know you. It must be on account of my illness, which they tell me has been terribly long."

"The longest I have ever heard of," answered Harry. "That you have recovered at all is, I think, little less than a miracle."

Dick scanned Harry's face for a full minute ere he spoke again.

"I should say that you are not my master," he said, "only I know that before I was ill I was in Paris with you, and I am there still."

"And suppose I am not your old master, but one of his blood—how would you bear that, Dick?"

"He had a younger brother," answered Dick, "but he was killed three years ago."

Here Dr. Leclerc came forward and took Dick's wrist between his finger and thumb. In a little while he said—

"You may tell him everything. He is strong enough to bear it."

"Dick," said Harry, "I am not your old master, but his son."

"His *son* ?"

The intensity of the ejaculation made Harry start and look at the doctor, who made no warning sign, and he went on—

"Yes, his son. You were injured years ago when abroad with my father, and you have been in a state of mind that changed you sorely. Now you have been restored by the marvellous skill of our good friend the physician here."

"And what have I been doing all this time ?" asked Dick.

"Living upon the moor—a nomad life—going here and there as you willed, but always with your heart turned to the Moated Grange."

"I have a little gipsy blood in my veins," said Dick, dreamily.

"Shall I go on ?"

"Yes, sir."

Then Harry in brief told him of the events we recorded in the earlier part of the story, reserving only recent events. He was not disposed to trust even the doctor with the story of the vengeance he had exercised upon his foes.

"That will do for to-night," said Dr. Leclerc, interposing. "To morrow, if you are still well enough, you may tell your own story. Meanwhile a composing draught will not hurt you."

He drew a small phial from his pocket and put a portion of its contents into a glass, adding some water.

He handed it to Dick, who, like an obedient child, drank it off. In a few minutes he was sound asleep.

"It would not have been well for him to think much to-night," said Dr. Leclerc ; "and now his mind and body will have unbroken rest for twelve hours at least. To-morrow, if he awakes as I hope he will be composed and refreshed, and able to impart to you the secrets you are so longing to hear."

"You guess there are secrets for him to tell me ?"

"I am sure, my friend, that there are mighty matters to be put before you by this man. I am skilled in reading the minds of others, although they are no affair of mine. Good-night !"

CHAPTER XVIII.

STORK AND CLEWSON—A QUARREL BETWEEN OLD ASSOCIATES— SWIVELS IN TROUBLE.

IN a chamber at the back of a low wine-shop in the doubtful region of St. Antoine three men were conversing together. The tone was not a friendly one, and high words were gathering like an increasing hailstorm.

The trio are known to the reader as Clewson, Stork, and Swivels, and the theme on which two at least had grown warm, was that of Harry Dalton and Dick.

"It is a question," said Clewson, "whether they are to perish or we to suffer. On you, Stork, rests the whole thing."

"And I," sulkily replied Stork, "tell you that I will have nothing more to do with the business. Whether you like it or not, I am going to the old country to-morrow."

"And I say that if you attempt it you will never reach its shores," rejoined Clewson, fiercely.

"Why can't we all go ?" whined Swivels.

"Silence, you drivelling hound !" said Clewson.

"Now, Stork, listen to me. If you will undertake what the prince desires to be done you will henceforth be a free man. A liberal sum of money will be paid to you, on which you will be able to live in the old country at ease."

"Who is to pay it ?" asked Stork, with a growl.

"The prince."

"And he as poor as a rat. No, and if he were as rich as a Jew banker I would not have anything to do with it. I haven't any spite against young Dalton myself, and he did me a good turn the other night. Go to the hotel yourself."

"I can't," answered Clewson ; "I am a marked man—not only there, but in Paris throughout. Take heed how you go against us."

"Who is to blow upon me ?" asked Stork.

"I will," replied Clewson, "this very night."

Stork looked at him steadily for a few moments, and the eyes of the other gazed upon him unflinchingly.

"Clewson," said Stork, "I've done you many a service in my life ; do me one now. Let me go away in peace."

"Hang your services," replied Clewson, roughly. "Do as you are told."

Stork, who had his right hand in the pocket of his coat, suddenly drew it out, and springing to his feet threw himself upon Clewson.

An oath or two was exchanged, then a blow was struck by Stork, and Clewson was lying on the floor gasping for breath.

The terrified Swivels, in a shaky way, endeavoured to throw himself between them, but Stork, having dealt the blow, seized him by the throat and cast him to the floor, where he lay half stunned.

The poacher cast a grim look at the pair, and tossing the knife he had used to the ground, walked out of the room.

He was as cool as if he had parted with them in the usual way, and strolled into the public room, where a number of men were drinking and discussing the hardness of their lot.

The landlord and his wife—a coarse pair, bloated with indulgence in drink—were serving a man who stood by the counter, and listening to a story he was telling them of the latest crime perpetrated in the so-called Queen of Cities.

"Friend," said Stork to the landlord, "there is a row going on in the back room with those two fellows. You had better stop it."

"How now!" exclaimed the landlord, "a row, and in my respectable wine-shop? Hey! then I stop him."

He picked up a stout stick from a corner of the bar—one that he kept as a peacemaker among the rough customers he had to deal with—and grimly dived under the flap of the counter.

"They are only accursed Englishmen," remarked his wife. "Spare them not."

"It shall be so, my loved one," he replied.

A powerful man and a resolute one, he was no mean person to tamper with, especially where he had one of the hated foes of his nation to deal with.

As he opened the door of the room Swivels was in the act of rising from the ground in a state of terror and dismay. Clewson was dead.

"So," cried the landlord, "you haf quarelled; and vhat is dis—a dead man? Stand!"

"Let me go!" moaned Swivels. "I have nothing do with it. Stork stabbed him."

"I tell you to stand," said the landlord, and then, as the trembling Swivels still made efforts to get by him, he dealt him a tremendous blow with his stick.

It scattered the senses of the miserable villain, and for a time he lost consciousness. When he came round he found the room was filled with people, and he was in the hands of the gendarmes, who had been summoned by the landlord.

"That it should happen here," said that worthy, "in my most respectable shop! It is too bad. Away with him to the guillotine!"

"I did not do it!" yelled Swivels, writhing in the grasp of the officers; "I swear it. Where is that Stork? It was he who struck the blow. They were quarrelling. I am innocent."

"Poof!" said the landlord, "it is a lie."

"Who are these men?" asked one of the gendarmes.

There were three of them, and they all held Swivels as if he had been a modern Samson.

"I know them not," replied the landlord. "They come to me and say, 'Give us a room and wine to drink,' and, behold! it is done. But I suspect, and say to my loving wife, 'I like not him of the rouge nose. He hath the aspect of a shedder of blood.' And, see, it is there."

"Away with him!" screamed the spectators, men who had come from the public room when the murder was made known by the excited landlord.

"I tell you I am innocent," said Swivels, shaking as if he had the ague. "Go after Stork."

"Zere is no Storks," replied the landlord, complacently; "I see him not. It is I who suspect, and come to stop ze murdare; but it was for me to be too late."

He was keen enough to know that he ought to have detained Stork in the first instance, and therefore he was determined, as a matter of self-protection to ignore him.

He would also gain some credit in the eyes of the officials, of which he was much in need, for having suspected a possible murder by him of the red nose. It was true that he had been too late, but as he said, "it was so difficult for him to leave the bar when many were clamouring to be served with his excellent wine."

Swivels, finding that all his declarations of innocence were ignored, relapsed into a state of utter despair, and was dragged from the wine-shop limp and verging upon a helpless condition.

A howling, raging, tearing mob accompanied him to the nearest station, but he scarcely heard the chaos of sounds around him.

Stunned by the awful nature of his position, and the helplessness that would prevent his clearing himself from the charge, for he had not a friend in the world to whom he could appeal, he could find no answers to the questions put to him by the chief officer, and was finally cast into a cell, dazed with terror, to await an examination in the court on the following morning.

CHAPTER XIX.

DICK TELLS HIS STORY—TOM STARBUCK AT THE HOTEL— FLIGHT OF THE PRINCE.

IN accordance with the prognostications of the doctor Dick slept about twelve hours and then awoke. He looked stronger and better than he had hitherto done, and on seeing Harry seated by his side gave him a respectful good-morning.

"I am almost well now, sir," he said, as if he were renewing a conversation broken off a few moments before, "and if there is anything you wish to know about your father I am ready to tell you."

"After you have had some refreshment," said the nurse, who was seated on the other side of the bed.

Some tea and light food was ordered for him, of which he partook sparingly, and then the nurse left master and man together.

"I want you," said Harry, "to go back to the time when you were abroad with my father."

"It is hardly going back," replied Dick, "for I feel as if it were but yesterday."

"Tell the story in your own way, then."

"I don't know that I can make everything clear to you," Dick began, "because I am not acquainted with everything; but all I have to tell you shall learn. Master, at the time we started for the Continent together, was a high-spirited young man, full of life and with not too much knowledge of the world. The soul of honour himself, he could not think meanly of others, and trusted everybody until he found them out.

"Now, sir, as we went here and there, we came across very strange people at times, but nobody to do us harm, until we got to Paris, and then things became unsettled. Master went into company I did not think much of, but then I was only a servant, and no judge of what was proper in a foreign land.

"There was a prince of the name of Vaubertie"—Harry started, but maintained silence—"who was one of the flashy sort, and his three brothers, all nice to look at, but, as I fancied, a lot of adventurers. There was a woman, too, whose name I never knew, and master was always about with her, driving in the Boulevards. Late hours were kept, and then came the night—the last of all I remember.

"Master told me he was going out," said Dick, thoughtfully, "and it entered my head that, as it was very late, he was going to some gambling place. He was not given that way, but he was easily led.

"I made up my mind to follow him—not out of curiosity, but with a dim idea that he might want me. I armed myself with a stout stick, which I was ready to use if it should be wanted. He walked that night, and he took a direction towards the Seine, and at last halted by a house on one of the quays.

"He knocked three times, and was admitted. I took up a position behind one of the buttresses of the wall of the river and waited. I suppose I must have been there an hour when the door opened, and two men came out carrying a dead body.

"The sight of it gave me a turn, for I thought surely it was my master; but as the men went by my hiding-place without noticing me I got a glimpse of the face, and saw it was one of the prince's brothers. I had learnt to know them all by sight.

"The men threw the body into the river and returned to the house. Almost as soon as the door was closed it was opened again, and two other men came out with a second body. I saw the face of that also, and it was another brother of the prince.

"Well, sir, to get on with the story, after a time the third brother was brought out, and master soon after followed. It seemed to me that he had been having a struggle with somebody, for his clothing was disarranged and he was flushed and heated. He was walking leisurely away when three men crept out of the house and rushed upon him. Here was the time when my services were needed, and I went to his aid.

"I can't give a full account of what followed. I only know that there was a fight and somebody dealt me a blow on the head which sent me down, and that is the end of my story."

"It is something, but not all I require," said Harry. "Can you suggest any other means of my getting at the full record of what had been going on?"

"Master kept a diary," replied Dick, after a moment's thought, "and he was in the habit of putting everything down in it."

"That, of course, was burnt with the Grange," said Harry, bitterly.

"I should say not, sir," returned Dick, "for he kept all his most precious papers in the uninhabited part of the Grange, which you tell me was not destroyed."

"It was intact when I came away," said Harry.

"Then, sir, it is safe, for nobody in those parts would think of ouching it believing it to be haunted. If we get away soon we might find all you want there."

"I will go when you are ready," said Harry, "and not before."

Dick was about to expostulate with him when they were interrupted by a knock at the door, and a servant, on being desired to enter, appeared.

"Major Starbuck and his son are below, monsieur," he said, "and wish to see you immediately."

———

CHAPTER XX.

THE MAJOR AND DICK—TOM STARBUCK AS A DETECTIVE.

HARRY walked to the public room, where he found the major and his son awaiting him. There were no other members of the public present, and therefore they could talk freely together.

"My dear Dalton, said the major, as they shook hands, "I have only just discovered you were in Paris. It was Tom who found you out."

"Saw you come in yesterday," murmured Tom, "and made inquiries. By the way, have you seen your old friend the prince?"

"Not lately," replied Harry, evasively.

"It seems to be all *up* with him," said Tom. "He and his daughter have vanished, and the police took possession of his house this morning."

"What has been discovered concerning him?" asked Harry, with a startled air.

"Ah! there you pip me," replied Tom. "The police, as usual,

are reticent. They order you off as soon as they see you, without giving you time to open your mouth."

"A bad lot—the prince," said the major, shaking his head.

"I think there was some good in the girl," observed Harry, thoughtfully ; "but she was no doubt under evil influence."

"A pretty face," remarked Tom, with a grin, "goes a long way in making a good character."

"It may have something to do with it in my case," assented Harry, smiling, "for I was much taken by her when first we met."

He then told them about the operation which Wild Dick had undergone, to which they listened attentively. Tom was especially interested.

"I wish Flowerpot could be operated on in the same way," said the boy ; "but his injuries are too deep-seated. He is a born fool."

"Come up and see the man who is at once my servant and friend," suggested Harry.

They went up with him to the room where Dick was lying. The moment the major appeared Dick started up in his bed and exclaimed—

"Mr. Starbuck !"

"Major Starbuck now," answered the major, kindly. "It is strange that you should remember me, for I am much altered."

"The face is nearly the same, sir, and the voice has not changed at all," said Dick.

They sat talking for awhile on matters of the past, which have no bearing on our story, and then Tom, tiring of it, announced that he was going for a stroll.

As it was his custom to take himself off at all times, the major made no objection, and the boy went below.

As he drew near the foot of the stairs he pulled up short. In the hall was the prince talking to one of the attendants, and the latter was saying—

"If it is monsieur's wish not to be announced it shall not be done."

"All I desire to know," returned the prince, "is how the sick man progresses. For the present it would not be well for him to know that so old and valued a friend as I am is in Paris. I understand that the doctor has forbidden all excitement ?"

"It is so, monsieur."

"Hence my anxiety to keep my presence here unknown. I will return and make further inquiry in a few days."

He slipped a coin into the hand of the man and glided out of the place.

Tom hesitated a few moments, then he followed him.

"There is mischief in the air," he thought, "and it will be my business to stop it if I can."

The prince, on leaving the hotel, lost no time in getting out of the busy thoroughfare into a side street. There he removed a hat he

THERE WAS A YELL FROM BELOW—SWIVEL HAD DROPPED UPON HOCKNIER.

was wearing and put on a fur cap, which changed his whole
appearance in a startling manner.

Possibly some facial distortion which he indulged in had something to do with it.

"In for a penny in for a pound," muttered Tom, as he kept
steadily on the track of the prince, who hastened away without
looking back.

The prince traversed street after street, like a man who has a
destination and meant to reach it with the least possible delay, and
soon it flashed upon Tom that he was making his way towards the
railway station.   The boy knew enough of the general surroundings
to have a fair idea of his bearings.

His surmise proved to be well founded, for presently the prince
reached the station for the coast lying north, and, entering it,
walked up to the ticket-office, around which a number of men were
crowding.

Tom got up behind the prince, with a bulky *bourgeois* as a screen,
and in due time heard him ask for a ticket for Calais.

The inference was clear.   The prince was flying from France,
and his destination was England.   His promise to return to the
hotel and make further inquiries was, therefore, a sham.

But why make any inquiry at all?

That was a nut Tom found much too hard for him to crack.

" Now what shall I do ?" he thought, "let him go, or kick up a
row and hand him over to the gendarmes ?   But what charge am I
to make against him ?   No, he had better be allowed to leave, and
if afterwards he should be wanted he could be easily got at."

He waited until he saw the prince seated in the train, which at
the appointed hour steamed out of the station, and then he
sauntered out and wandered about, gratifying his curiosity anent
the natives by watching them pursuing their daily avocations.

He was very fond of the quarters inhabited by the poorer classes,
and he was mooning about a perfect slum near the Seine when a
woman who came out of one of the houses attracted his attention.

She was of a very different mould, although poorly clad, to the
rest of the people about.   Her figure was graceful, and she walked
with the easy step of a well-bred woman.   Her face he could not
see, for she wore a thick veil.

She objected to Tom, or so he judged by her suddenly turning
from him and hastening away.   He followed her a short distance,
until she came to a by-street, down which she vanished.

When Tom got to the corner she was no longer in sight.

"I wonder who she is ?" muttered Tom.   " It is some girl I have
seen before—a lady's maid, I reckon, bent on some mission of
charity."

But whoever she was she had disappeared, and, dismissing her
from his mind, he sauntered back towards the hotel, " to pick up the
major," as he expressed it.

CHAPTER XXI.

A NEW NURSE—ON THE WAY HOME—THE LIGHT AT THE GRANGE.

WILD DICK, as we will call him for the last time, after several promising days, began to show signs of a relapse. He became rather feverish, and Dr. Leclerc for the first time since the apparent success of his operation was anxious.

"It is in the mind more than the body," he said, gravely, "where the evil lies."

"He is desirous of getting away from here as soon as possible," answered Harry.

"Then he must go. I would recommend Cannes."

"It is his old home he is thinking of," said Dick.

"Ah! that might be too far," mused the doctor. "For the present he must remain where he is."

It happened the next day that the nurse who had recently been with him was taken ill. It was only the outcome of excessive devotion to duty, but she was no longer fit for her post, and she had to go.

Then came the difficulty. From the society which had sent her, there were no more nurses available, nor did the doctor at the moment know where one could be got.

However, he came in the evening, saying he had found a suitab'e person, whose only fault was that she would not show her face, having taken a religious vow not to unveil it to a living person for a certain length of time.

"That is no great obstacle," said Harry. "Let her come."

So the woman came, and proved to be, in figure at least, rather a young and attractive person.

She was very quiet, speaking little, and then only in a tone so low that her voice, if it had not been singularly clear, would hardly have been heard.

She had, however, the virtue of a good nurse, and performed her duties quietly and well. Ere she had been many hours with Dick he was full of her praises.

"I should soon get well, sir," he said, during her temporary absence from the room, "if I could only have her nursing me in the old country."

"Could you bear the journey there?" asked Harry.

"I could bear anything but this city," answered Dick. "The memory of what I saw here and the suffering it has brought makes me hate the place."

"Then the journey shall be risked," said Harry.

But first of all, if only in courtesy, the doctor must be again consulted, and when he came on the morrow Harry put the question to him. The doctor, to his surprise, at once assented.

"Get him from here as soon as you can," he said.

Harry did not know that the good doctor, having justly vaunted his work in the press, was getting anxious not to have his patient die under his care. It would be so much better, professionally speaking, for him to pass away where the fact would not be talked about, and probably never heard of, among the savants who were the rivals of the clever operator.

So it was decided to start on the morrow.

"And you will take me back to the old Grange, won't you, sir?" pleaded Dick.

"Assuredly," answered Harry. "I will wire to the agent to have it prepared for our coming."

"Don t do that, sir," said Dick. "I've got a fancy for going back to it just as you left it. It is only a sick man's whim, but you will gratify it, I hope."

Of course Harry assented. It was all one to him.

Then came the question of the nurse. Would she go with them?

When the matter was mooted to her she simply said it was as well to be in one place as another, so long as she had her work to do. There was no definite change in her voice, but it did occur to Harry that she seemed pleased.

In response to a question about her luggage she said she had nothing more to take than the small portmanteau she had brought with her.

"But you will have to communicate with your society," urged Harry, "or to your sisterhood," with a glance at her dress, which was of a nun-like cut and material. "They will want to know where you are."

"I have neither society not sisterhood," she replied; "I am alone in the world."

He was puzzled, but as much depended on her going he said no more.

That night the major and Tom came again, and heard that Harry would be gone on the morrow.

"I shall go back to the old home and make myself busy for a time in restoring it," he told them.

"There is a fellow in England you had better fight shy of," advised Tom. "I mean the prince."

He informed Harry of the way he had come to learn of that mysterious man having gone to England, and Harry's brow darkened. He did not like the persistent way he haunted him, and it occurred to his mind that his departure might be of some personal interest to him.

"If I come across the prince," he said, "I will take steps to prevent his troubling me in the future."

"Do nothing rash, my boy," said the major. "Remember that at home no man is allowed to take the law into his own hands."

"I shall consider the country I am in very little," said Harry, "if I meet him in a quiet spot."

The major said no more just then, but on taking leave of Harry he went from the hotel, and outside made a very gratifying announcement to Tom.

"I am going on to England in the wake of that very impetuous young man. It is a duty I owe to the memory of his father and uncle—good fellows both. I shall put up somewhere near his home—I daresay there is an inn of some sort—and look out for a chance of being useful to him. If he has not somebody to steer him straight he will get into trouble."

So it fell out that Harry had two self-appointed guardian angels, and the time was not far off when he would need one or both of them.

It promised to be a trying journey to Dick, for when helped from his bed he could scarcely stand. He was as weak as a child, and the people of the hotel said good-bye to "monsieur the sick" as they would have taken leave of a friend going to execution.

"It is not for him to see the white land of his birth," said the head waiter. "It is a pity, but perhaps monsieur his master wishes for him to die."

Which showed exactly how much they knew of the true state of the case.

But it is not the servants of the hotel whom we have to think of —their opinion was of no consequence. Dick was taken to the station, where an invalid carriage had been provided for him. He bore the journey so well that he was able to walk on board the boat with the aid of the arm of the nurse.

"She is a good woman," he said to his master, as they sat on the deck of the steamer ploughing her way across the sea, "and so pretty."

"How do you know?" asked Harry.

"As we walked aboard, sir," whispered Dick, "the wind blew her veil a little aside, and I saw her face. It was pretty, but she looked as if she had suffered *and was the better for it.*"

Harry's curiosity was powerfully excited, but he did not feel justified in endeavouring to satisfy it. The secret of the nurse, whatever it might be, would be held sacred by him.

Still, he could not refrain from glancing at her at times as she sat apart from them quietly reading a book.

At intervals she came over to her patient to see if she could render him any service. When there was anything to be done she did it and returned to her seat, seldom uttering a word.

The passage was a smooth one, and that night they stayed at the Lord Warden at Dover. Harry was willing to remain there for awhile, but Dick was all for getting on.

"I shall not rest," he said, "until we are at the old place. You can't tell, sir, how I long to see it."

"As you will, Dick," was the reply.

The feeling of the man found little response in the master. Harry, now that he was in England, seemed to hang fire, and desired to avoid the Grange. He could not properly define the feeling, which was more of an indefinite premonition of coming evil than anything else.

But he was not of the stuff to yield to presentiments, and on the morrow they were on the move again, travelling, however, by road. Harry was resolved not to tax his faithful servant with a roundabout journey by rail.

It took time, and three days had elapsed when they sighted the moor, which was to Dick like a long-lost home.

"I can feel the sweet breeze," he said.   "There is no air to compare with it in the wide world."

"It seems to me to be heavier than it used to be," said Harry.

As the day was on the wane he decided to see what accommodation the Panting Deer could give him.   Harry had, for good reasons, no great love for the place, but the old landlord was gone, as he had learnt from his agent, and a more honest man had taken the place.

Of trade there was little, but the new tenant was one of the keepers of an adjacent deer forest, and was to an extent independent of it.

The man was considerably astonished to see a carriage drive up to the door and a gentleman bronzed with foreign travel descend from it.

Harry's identity was soon established, and although there were no rooms fit for guests, the keeper's wife promised to have some quickly prepared.

Dick was soon established in comfortable quarters, and Harry, in the bar, got into conversation with his host.

"I suppose you never go near the old Grange ?" he said.

"Nobody ever does, sir, if they can help it," was the man's reply "You see, sir, there be a yarn about its being haunted."

"What nonsense," exclaimed Harry.

"That used to be my opinion, sir."

"But isn't it now ?"

"Well, sir, it may be haunted by the living and not the dead, but somebody or something is there, or at least was there last night."

"Tell me what you mean," said Harry, "and why you name last night especially ?"

"Because I had to go pretty near the Grange about eleven o'clock, as I was coming from the forest," answered the keeper, "and I saw a light at one of the windows."

A frown darkened the brow of Harry.

"Some loafer intruding there, perhaps," he said.   "If so, he had better not be there to-night."

"Lor', sir, what if he is ?"

"He will have to answer to me for the intrusion."

"If I was you, sir," said the keeper, slowly, "I should let the old place go.   It aint brought much luck to you or yours for many a day."

"I shall be there to-night," replied Harry, resolutely, "get dinner ready as quick as you can.   I will go alone.   Say nothing to my people."

"As you like, sir, of course," said the keeper.   "I'd go with you but for being bound to work round on the other side of the moor.

The stags have got their fighting fit on them, and we have to see that they don't stray."

"I should not think of troubling you," rejoined Harry. "I know my way into the place, and have a key that opens a door that was private in my father's time—it escaped the fire."

He returned to Dick, who, with the nurse, was in one of the back rooms, where a cheerful fire was burning. He talked with him until dinner was announced, and then left him.

The nurse followed him outside the room.

"I should like to speak to you," she said, in her now familiar soft tone of voice.

"Yes," responded Harry. "What is it you want?"

"Nothing," she said, "save to warn you. I am a believer in dreams, and of late I have had very bad ones. You have been often in them, and I beg of you not to wander abroad too much alone."

"I thank you," said Harry, "but I have nothing to fear. This is my own country."

"It does not follow it is safe for all that," she replied. "I know you are brave and do not feel fear like other men, but still I would have you take heed even of a foolish woman's warning."

He smiled and thanked her, at the same time declaring that there was nothing to fear.

She said no more, but with a sigh left him.

He waited until dusk ere he started for the Grange, leaving the house at the same time as the keeper.

Their ways lay different, but they stopped outside to exchange a few words ere they parted.

"If I am late," said Harry, "there will be no difficulty about getting in, I suppose?"

"No, sir," replied the keeper; "the missus will sit up for you."

"If I am not back by the morning," continued Harry, "will it be troubling you too much to come over to see the reason I am delayed?"

"Not at all, sir. I am not afeard of coming there in daylight."

They parted, and Harry, with his quick, strong stride, stepped out across the moor.

The coming night promised to be a dark one, for it was clouding up. There was a probability of rain, and the wind was rising.

It was not the night the majority of people would have selected for an expedition to a lonely, deserted house with an uncanny reputation, but no fears entered into the calculation of Harry. He was eager to commence the search for the diary of his father, which Dick was almost sure he would find in one of the rooms of the oldest and only remaining portion of the mansion.

He also wanted to know if there was an intruder within its walls.

As he hastened on the darkness rapidly fell, and the gathering clouds grew deeper. A stranger to moor life would have had some difficulty in picking his way through the growth of stunted bushes and the occasional heaps and scattered masses of broken stones.

But to Harry the way was familiar.   He could have traversed the moor blindfolded, avoiding the obstacles by instinct, or guided by the nature of the soil, which told him what lay immediately ahead of him.

When about two-thirds of the journey had been performed everything a short distance away was lost to view.   He halted to make sure of the direction he was taking, looking above to catch a glimpse of the stars through one of the openings still to be found in the masses of clouds.

Having got his bearings, he resumed his way, and a few minutes later he had a further guide.   A light flashed out ahead.

"There is somebody in the Grange," he muttered, and with his face set with anger he hurried on.

.   .   .   .

At the same hour there were other arrivals at the Panting Deer in the form of two persons—the major and his son Tom.   They came on horseback and alone.

They did not expect to find anyone there, having been informed that no guests ever visited the house.

It was, therefore, with a feeling akin to alarm that the major heard of the coming of Harry and his two companions.

"But the young squire has gone on to the Grange," said the keeper's wife, "and he will not be back until late."

She showed them into a room, and went off to get the materials for a fire.   The major paced uneasily up and down.

"I would rather have found him here," he said, "although it might have been awkward.   That story we heard about lights being seen in the Grange makes me think that there are possibly dangerous characters in the place.   I have a good mind to follow him."

"Dad," said Tom, "you have been out in the jungle alone at night—surely you could find your way across the moor."

"If I knew the direction to take, my son."

"You can inquire about that."

"Tom," said the major, resolutely, "I'll do it.   Although I am not superstitious I have been bothered all day with uneasy thoughts about Harry Dalton.   I owe the family something, and it will please me much if I can repay it.   I will be off to the Grange and you can go to bed."

"Certainly, dad," replied Tom, demurely, as he turned round and privately winked at the wall.   If the major went Tom did not mean to be very far behind him.

CHAPTER XXII.

THE MAJOR AND HIS SON ARE IN THE NICK OF TIME—THE FINDING OF THE DIARY.

MAJOR STARBUCK armed himself before setting out with a pair of revolvers and a stout malacca cane with a heavy ivory top. Although no longer a young man, he was still, thus provided, a match for an ordinary opponent.

The night was dark, and it was raining, but with the moon behind the clouds it was not so absolutely black but that a man accustomed to travelling in the country could pick his way.

He knew the direction he ought to take, and having set his face towards it strode onward at a good pace.

Barely had he left the inn when young Tom appeared, also armed with a revolver, which his father did not know he was the possessor of, and as an additional means of defence he bore in his hand a short, heavy life-preserver, likewise an unrevealed piece of private property.

The boy had the good eyesight of the young, and he also had the coolness of one of more advanced years.

He had known what it was to travel at night in countries where the only lights known after sunset were the moon and stars, or the occasional fire of some traveller resting in the open for the night.

So they went on together, the major pausing at times to make sure that he was going in the right direction, until they came within easy hail of the Moated Grange, in which, as they drew near, a light was seen burning.

Now the major knew nothing of the structure of the building, but he was aware that part of it had been destroyed, while the old portion as yet remained intact.

How to get into it was a problem.

He found around the outside of it a mass of stone-work, the ruins of the portion of the building burnt down by the fire. On his right loomed out the turrets and towers still standing.

A break in the clouds came suddenly and helped him. Clambering over the irregular pile of rubbish, he cast a glance around, and saw the doorway, which was open.

Beyond it was a dark passage, which he entered, and found himself at the foot of a stone staircase.

Up he went, feeling his way step by step, to the top.

As he paused on the level to take breath he fancied he heard something moving in the darkness ahead of him.

It was as if someone was creeping cautiously along, and there was also a sound of a hand drawn across stonework, as if the person was feeling his way.

He knew it could not be Harry Dalton, as he would have gone anywhere in a bolder fashion, so he stood still and listened.

Tom, who was not far behind his father, pulled up too, and, listening with all his ears, heard the suppressed breathing of the major a few feet away. Afterwards he also detected the slight noise made by the unknown person further on.

As they both stood there a door was opened without a sound, and a band of light streamed out. Then they saw the form of a man, whom they recognised as the Prince Vaubertie, peering into a chamber furnished with ancient fittings and drapery, bearing the signs of long neglect.

Another person was evidently inside, and they guessed it was Harry Dalton. The prince drew out a revolver and took aim.

Then, with a shout, the major rushed forward and struck the would-be murderer a heavy blow with the Malacca cane. He staggered, but did not fall.

Quick as lightning he faced about and fired.

The bullet went so near the head of the major that he involuntarily ducked. There was a hasty movement in the chamber, and the occupant rushing forward revealed that it was indeed Harry who was there.

As he came boldly to the door, with a candle in his right hand and a revolver in the left, the prince turned to fly.

In the gloom he dashed against the major, and, upsetting him, would have got away but for Tom, who, seeing all that had happened, prepared for action. As the prince passed him he struck him on the head with his life-preserver.

The blow was a telling one, and it was delivered just as the running man reached the head of the stairs. Without a moan he went headlong down.

"Hurrah! I've nobbled him," shouted Tom.

"What is going on there?" asked Harry, as he appeared in the passage.

Then, seeing the major in the act of rising, and Tom capering about, he uttered an exclamation of surprise.

"*You* here," he said, "and using a revolver?"

"It wasn't the governor," said Tom, "but that fellow, the prince, whom I have sent down to the bottom of the stairs. He won't get up in a hurry, for I landed on the cranium."

The expression of the major's face as he stared at his son was worth a long journey to see.

"What the deuce brought you here, you young imp?" he growled.

"Came to help you," replied Tom, complacently, "and as things have turned out you wanted me badly."

"I knew somebody was in the place, or was here a short time ago," said Harry, "for I saw a light, but on entering I failed to find any trace of him. I thought it might be some poacher who had been skulking here for a time. It is the prince, you say, Tom?"

"Yes, I know the beggar," answered the boy, "and you will find him below. I rather fancy I have stopped his capering for awhile."

Harry, holding the light aloft, descended the stairs, the major and his son following. Half-way down they came upon the form of the prince, lying head downmost on the stairs.

He was unconscious, but breathing hard, like one suffering from an attack of apoplexy. They raised him up and sat him against the wall.

At first there was no sign of the injury he had received, but Harry, on closer examination, discovered an indentation on the top of his head.

"Just where poor Dick was wounded years ago," he said, wonderingly.

There was silence for a few moments, and then the major remarked, quietly—

"It is very strange. I am not one to assume or deny that there are especial acts of judgment for such a man as this, but really it looks like it."

"We had better carry him upstairs," said Harry, "and see if there is anything that can be done for him."

He gave the light to Tom, and the two men bore the insensible form of the prince back to the room above.

It had been a drawing-room in the olden time, and some mildewed lounges were there. They laid him upon one of them, and the major examined the injury he had received.

"Bad," was the first comment he made. "It won't kill him, but it will take two Dr. Leclercs to put him right again."

"There is no doctor within miles of this place," observed Harry. "Nothing can be done for him until morning. We can only let him lie there."

"I do not know that he has any great claim on your consideration," remarked the major, "seeing that he has just now made an attempt upon your life."

"Not for the first time," replied Harry. "He must have got an inkling of my arrival here to-night and hid himself away until he thought he had a fair chance of assassinating me."

This was a reasonable assumption, and probably the correct one ; but it was a matter they would never be enlightened upon, for the prince had lost the light of the world for ever.

For him there was to be, as there had been for Dick, the darkness of the mind that obliterates the past and mars the future, only in a more accentuated form. Absolute idiocy was to be his lot.

"And to think that I did it after all !" thought Tom. "Well, I am not going to bother about it, for it just serves him right."

Turning away from the prostrate man, Harry told the object of his being there that night.

"My father, I have every reason to believe," he said, "left a diary, which will, if I find it, assuredly enlighten me as to the mystery of his acquaintance with this man, which, as I have told you, led to the assassination of him and my poor brother. As we must remain here for some hours, will you kindly help to search for it ?"

The major was only too willing to help him in any way, and Tom also, so they set about the work together.

Harry, it seemed, had only just begun the search, and as yet had found nothing beyond evidence that the supposed deserted part of the Grange had undoubtedly been frequented by somebody during the years immediately before the double murder and the burning described in the opening of our story.

It was not so long ago, after all, and the torn papers and other things illustrative of the doings of a busy man were still comparatively fresh upon the floor.

Harry examined some of the fragments, but found nothing that could be construed into a portion of a diary. Then a thorough examination of the furniture of the room was made, but they discovered not the remotest thing of a helpful nature.

"If the diary is anywhere it is in another room," said Harry.

From the chamber they went to several apartments. In some there was a little furniture in a state of neglect and decay, others were empty, and it was not until they came to the top of one of the high turrets that they discovered anything of interest.

There they found a door which was locked, but Harry put his shoulder to it, and the woodwork of the lintels being rotten, it soon yielded to the pressure.

On making their way in they saw that it had been occupied as a sort of study, being furnished with a secretaire and writing-chairs, and fitted up with shelves, on which were a few books.

It was to the secretaire Harry first directed his attention.

It was locked, but he succeeded in breaking open the top drawer, and the first thing he saw was a parchment-covered book about a foot deep and eight or nine inches wide.

On the cover of it was an inscription, which Harry read by the light of the candle held up by Tom. It ran as follows :—

"MY DIARY.—To be read by my sons after my death."

"I have it now," remarked Harry, drawing a deep breath ; "but I shall make no attempt to read it here."

"No, indeed," assented the major. "Sit down and have a cigar with me—you want something to soothe you—and let us talk of other things."

"I could do with a soother, too," murmured Tom.

But his father only looked at him by way of reply, and Tom had to solace himself without a weed.

———

CHAPTER XXIII.

THE CONTENTS OF THE DIARY.

EARLY in the morning the major returned to the inn, and, mounting his horse, rode over to a distant town to fetch a doctor.

By noon the man of medicine was at the Grange, and his verdict was final.

"This man may live on many years, but he will never have his wits again."

Then the police were summoned and the affair explained to

them.   The fact that the prince had no right at the Grange was sufficient confirmation, and no trouble was anticipated in that direction.   Pending the return of the prince to his senses they could do nothing.

And of a surety they did not desire to move, for the family of the Daltons were held in high esteem all through the county, the retiring habits of Harry's father to the contrary notwithstanding.

Up to this time Harry had not looked at the diary, but on the prince being taken away to the far-off town infirmary he returned to the inn.   After a brief interview with Dick he sought a private room which had been prepared for him, and there began the task of reading the diary.

It was not so voluminous as it appeared to be from the outside, but there was still a copious amount of matter in it.

In the first part he dwelt upon family matters pure and simple, and it was not until he arrived at the twenty-fourth page that Harry Dalton came to the part of the journal which had such an absorbing interest for him.

We need not give dates, and will confine ourselves to extracts.

"In Paris.   . . .   As yet know nobody, but to-day was spoken to by a man of undoubtedly good breeding. .. . .   I was outside a café ; he sat down by my side, and talked European politics.

"Met my agreeable acquaintance again to-day.   He gave me his card, which showed that he was Prince Vaubertie.   Have heard of the family. . . .   Rather fancy that their record is not good, but won't be sure.

" Spent the evening with the prince in a gambling saloon.   Shady company.   Asked him how he came to mix with such people, and he only laughed.   One and all treated him too familiarly. . . . Refused to gamble, having no taste that way. . . .

" A strange night.   Was at home at my hotel, when the prince called with his two younger brothers.   Both handsome, agreeable fellows.   Went again to the gambling saloon. . . .

" A large party there, and words arose through a stranger to me quarrelling with the prince.   Strong language was used, and accusations were bandied to and fro.   I heard some strange things— among others that I was in a den of murderers and thieves, a portion of a band spread all over the Continent.   It was headed by the prince, who had nothing but his name to live upon.   The quarrelsome member was stabbed behind his back.   I tried to leave, but was detained. . . .

. . . .

"And now I come to a terrible part of my life. . . .   It is three days since I entered a line in my diary, and they have been passed in watching beside the bed of my faithful valet, who has received a blow from which I fear he will never recover sufficiently to support me in a story I should be glad to tell to the police. . .

" In the first place, let me go back to the night when I saw the murder committed in the gambling saloon.   I tried to leave, as I have written before, but was stopped, and an oath of allegiance to the gang of thieves and murderers demanded of me. . . .

"I refused to take it, and then came a short debate as to what was to be done with me. Some were for shooting me down as I stood, but there were a few who were willing to give me a chance for life, and they prevailed. . . .

"The chance was a poor one. I had to fight each member of the band in turn, and kill them all ere I could be free. . . .

"It seemed that they had a rule on the subject, and it was now put into force. . . . I was given a sword and allowed to select my first opponent. . . . Having been lured into the den by the prince and his brothers, I turned to them and selected the youngest. . . . I feared that I had no prospect of escaping with my life, and I resolved to kill as many as possible. . . .

"I saw the lip of the prince quiver, for he was fond of this younger brother in his way, and when we stood up facing each other his eyes were dim with anxiety. He had heard me speak of myself as a fairly expert swordsman. . . .

"I killed him. . . . It was only the work of a few moments. . . . A feint—a turn of the wrist, and he was on the floor, with the life-blood welling from his breast. . . . There was no uproar in the room, and some of their number picked him up and carried him out. . . .

"I was allowed three minutes' rest and a glass of wine. . . . After that I made my next selection, and chose the other brother of the prince. . . . He dare not refuse, and we faced each other for a brief space of time, with the same result. . . . I killed him also. . . .

"It was as they were carrying the second of the dead men out that the prince fell upon me. It is probable that he lost his head, and came at me in a blind fury. . . . I was in the act of drinking, but my eye was upon him, and, eluding the thrust he intended for my heart, I knocked him down and made for the door. . . .

"It was a sanguinary fight, and I must have left half a score dead or wounded in the passage, but I got to the open air, and although a few of the most desperate—among them the prince—clung to me they soon let go and fled. I was conscious during the last few moments of the struggle that I was being helped by somebody, but I did not know it was my servant Dick until he and I were left alone. He was then lying on the ground apparently dead. . . .

"I picked him up and carried him to a surgeon's house, guided by the red lamp over the door. He said at once that my faithful servant would be an idiot or in some way insane for the term of his natural life. . . .

"I remained in Paris, and I told my story to the police. . . . They laughed at me. . . . The prince and his brother, I was informed, left Paris two days before. . . . I was evidently considered insane, and they were disposed to put the injuries of my servant upon me. . . .

"Not even at the British Embassy could I get any help. There they would not have anything to do with the matter, and plainly intimated that it was entirely an affair for the police. . . . So I went home, taking poor Dick with me, and from that time resolved to go no more abroad. . . ."

Then followed at intervals, among other things, accounts of threatening letters, to the effect that the family of the Daltons would one day be exterminated, and how that threat was nearly carried out we know.

Harry arose from the perusal of the book with a certain sense of relief, for now he knew all, and much that had been so mysterious was made clear to him.

The retired life of his father was in part accounted for, and if he did not personally fear the league he was at least prudent in keeping as well as he could out of their way.

Harry called to mind how, in his early days, he had been carefully guarded as he walked abroad, but as time passed the vigilance was diminished.

Years had not relaxed the bitterness of the prince, and he must—at intervals, at least—have set a watch upon the Grange. When a favourable time arrived to strike his emissaries were sent to do the dastard work.

But, although in part done, the punishment which had fallen on them was complete. All but one were dead, or in a condition never to trouble again. Harry was sure of that.

And it may here be said they never did.

Swivels was found guilty of a crime he had not committed and sent to the galleys for life, the jury having found extenuating circumstances in his case.

Better for him if they had not, for then he would have gone to the guillotine and been put out of his misery, instead of dragging on a wearisome and loathsome existence for many years.

Stork was never more heard of, but a poacher in the north, who was slain in an affray with keepers, bore so strong a resemblance to him that his fate may be considered practically certain.

Dick was in feeble health for a time, but he eventually rallied and became strong enough to go a voyage in the Mediterranean with his master and the two Starbucks.

Flowerpot, who had been vegetating for awhile, was also of the party, and was a good and faithful servant until they put in at Malta. There he disappeared with his master's jewellery for three days, and was found hopelessly drunk just as he had got rid of the proceeds of his nefarious conduct.

He was sent to a military prison for a year, and the major wisely in future chose one of his own countrymen to serve him.

There is one person of whom we have yet to say a word, and that is the nurse who waited on Dick so sedulously.

She remained behind when Harry Dalton went abroad, and obtained a situation in the asylum where the prince was confined. There she remained for two years, until his death, and then she went away in spite of the inducements offered her to remain.

She proceeded to London, and worked in the hospitals there for a time. They said of her that she was the best of nurses, but one day she was missing, and never returned.

There was a reason for her absence, and it was this.

She was passing by St. George's Church, Hanover-square, as a wedding party came out. The bride was a charming girl—a daughter of one of our noblest families—and the bridegroom a tall, handsome man, bronzed with travel.

She knew him at a glance. It was Harry Dalton.

All through her life as a nurse she had worn a veil when abroad, and sometimes, as we know, when she was on duty. It was down now, and it hid the dreadful pallor in her face.

She turned away, and with an unfaltering step sought a modest lodging she occupied when not at the hospital, situated in a quiet part of Camden Town. She complained to her landlady of being in need of rest, and asked to let her lie undisturbed until the morrow.

She went to her bed, but not to sleep. For hours her white face grew whiter, and then at last there was a strange shadow of a coming change upon it. She folded her hands upon her breast and murmured—

"It is just. I was never worthy of him, and he would not have loved me long. May my poor blessing rest upon his life."

And when the morrow came, and the landlady of the house, not hearing her lodger stirring, went into the room, she was shocked to find her dead.

The handsome face was still, and the repose of death added to its beauty.

"She looked like an angel," the landlady afterwards said.

Let us hope that with all her faults she is one. In the latter part of her life she did her best to atone for many sins.

It was Aurora Vaubertie.

THE END.